CELEBRATING TINA

STRYKER SECURITY FORCE - BOOK 3

SARA BLACKARD

Copyright © 2020 Sara Blackard
For more information on this book and the author visit: https://www.sarablackard.com

Edited by Sweetly Us Press

All rights reserved.

No part of this book may be reproduced in any form or by any electronic or mechanical means, including information storage and retrieval systems, without written permission from the author, except for the use of brief quotations in a book review.

ONE

Tina West breathed in the crisp mountain air, relishing the frosty nip on her cheeks. The mountains stood still and silent, except for the frantic crunching of snow her Belgian Malinois, Scout, made as he dashed through the trees. Could the forest feel her grief? Was it absent of its normal squirrels' chatter and bird song in mourning with her? She closed her eyes and inhaled deeply, letting the sorrow wash over her — galvanize her to remember why she was out here training Scout when she could be back at the ranch having Thanksgiving dinner with the rest of the Stryker crew.

This Thanksgiving was the first one in four years that she'd thought she might move past the horror and hurt the holiday always brought. She should've known she couldn't escape the memories.

Tina huffed, swiping the tears that cooled her cheeks even more. How she wished she could go back in time and pay attention. To notice something that would have told her what her foster dad had been doing to her sister. Fruitless wish since time travel was impossible.

Scout whined at her feet, pushing his head against her hand. It was strange how animals could sense your emotions. She forced a smile as she scratched behind his ear.

"Come on, Scout." She motioned with her hand. "Let's get going."

Scout took off through the snow, bounding like a deer. He stumbled, rolled into the knee-deep snow and popped out covered in white. Joy bubbled up Tina's throat and spilled out, filling the silence with the lighthearted sound. A squirrel protested the intrusion from the trees, further breaking the melancholy. Yep, she needed this. Needed the focus of training Scout so they could be the best search team in Colorado, helping those lost and doing her part in taking down evil people.

She rushed after her dog, her snowshoes crunching in the crusty snow. She pushed herself faster through the trees. When she had woken up with her stomach twisting and revolting at the thought of food and people, she'd moved up her training excursion.

Her boss Zeke hadn't been happy, the grumpy slash of his eyebrows comical as Eva, his fiancee's daughter, had twirled circles around him. Rafe, the resident gadget geek, had loaded her down with enough gear to survive the apocalypse, and Derrick, aka Mother Goose, had made her promise to check in no later than 1500 hours as he'd double checked her gear Rafe had just finished repacking.

The attention had jabbed her tattered heart, like

suturing a wound without numbing the area first. It pulled and hurt, leaving her exhausted though she'd just gotten up.

Yet, the overprotective treatment also left her feeling more together than she had in years. Like maybe she had found a family not monstrous to its core. Somehow she'd landed herself smack dab in the middle of a clan of friends that had adopted her as their little sister. It left her full and uncomfortable. How could she ever trust after all that had happened to her?

She slowed as she came to an overlook, her breath fogging in front of her face in choppy puffs.

She scanned over the top of the snow-covered trees into the valley below. While beautiful, the icy scene made her wonder if she would always freeze out others. Always keep them at a distance. She didn't want to end up like the ice queen in one of Eva's fairy tale books, cold and loveless.

"Get a grip, Tina."

Scout cocked his head at her as if questioning her sanity.

Tina laughed. "I know. I'm wondering if I'm crazy, too."

She pulled up her sleeve and glanced at her watch. Rolling her eyes, she plopped her pack in the snow at her feet and snatched the sat phone Rafe had forced on her.

"Time to check in with Goose." Tina smiled at Scout. Derrick's dreadful nickname was perfect for the man who constantly triple checked everything and everyone.

Scout hung his tongue out and grinned. She still couldn't believe Zeke had brought the dog home for her, saying he'd be the perfect addition to the Stryker team if she was willing to train him. She'd fallen instantly in love with the idea and the dog and had spent the last month training almost non-stop when she wasn't watching Eva.

Tina leaned against a jumble of boulders and dialed home, pulling a miniature candy cane from her pocket. The little candies were the only good thing about the holidays. Scanning the terrain below, she searched for where she could pop her tent for the night. A breeze teased the ends of her hair and rattled the naked aspen branches. The quiet of the backcountry settled on her, almost suffocating her with its emptiness.

Maybe camping alone wasn't the brightest idea, especially on this day. The ghosts of her past might assault her more in her solitude than she had originally considered. A chill skated down her coat collar, sliding along her warm skin. She shivered as the call connected.

"Hey, Tiny Tina." Rafe's teasing voice came through the phone. "How's the training going?"

Tina huffed at the annoying nickname. She couldn't help that she had stopped growing at five foot two. While she wasn't thrilled with the name, it was another stitch that sutured her to the Stryker family.

"It's going great. Scout is taking to the snow." Tina chuckled at Scout rolling on the frozen ground like he was in heaven. "It's gorgeous back here."

Clicking came through the phone, followed by Rafe's low whistle. "According to the GPS, you've gone over fifteen miles already."

"Really?" The number both energized and tired her. *Sore muscles, here I come.*

"Listen, we just got word that there is a backcountry skier that hasn't checked in." Rafe sighed. "His GPS tracker last reported him in your area. The police chief didn't sound too concerned when I called to get info, but the guy's mom is freaking out."

Rafe snickered, causing Tina to grin. Being ex-special forces, the men at Stryker Security weren't the most coddling, unless it was Eva. That four-year-old had all those mighty warriors clutched in her teeny grasp.

"Has S & R been called out yet?" Tina poured water in the collapsible bowl for Scout as her pulse ramped up with both excitement and worry.

What if she didn't find the skier? What if she and Scout wandered right past him?

"Nah, not until tomorrow," Rafe answered.

"All right. We'll start looking."

"Look, this guy probably just broke his GPS, and he'll show up in time for his mommy's pumpkin pie." Rafe's tone, while joking, held a hint of warning to it. "Don't compromise your safety for someone we're not even sure needs rescuing."

Tina ruffled, but forced a laugh. "Watch out, Rafe, or I'll start calling you Goose."

"Psht, whatever. I just know you, and you'll help others while putting yourself at risk."

"And you guys don't?"

"We've trained for the last decade. You haven't."

Tina rolled her eyes.

"And before you get all bent out of shape, I'm just saying be careful." Rafe huffed, and Tina could picture him smoothing down his hair in his exasperation. "I like having a little sister around to pester again."

Hookay. Tina's nose stung, and she blinked to keep the tears at bay.

"I'll be careful." She cleared her throat. "What's the guy's name?"

"Milo Bishop. He's a cop here in town." Rafe's words had her heart racing again.

It couldn't be the Milo Bishop, her secret crush her freshman year. He was too capable, too larger-than-life to get lost in the woods. She capped her water bottle, ignoring the way her hands trembled.

"Got it. I'll check in if I find him, otherwise, I'm planning on setting up camp before dark, then heading out in the morning."

"Copy that. Keep alert. I wouldn't want the mountain lions to eat you. Sweet dreams, Tasty Tina." Rafe laughed, then hung up the phone.

Tina covered her eyes with her hand and shook her head. Had he just called her Tasty Tina? Tina's gaze darted behind her, then scanned the trees. Her heart beat wildly in her chest at Rafe's joke. Of course, mountain lions roamed the area, but surely they wouldn't get close with Scout around. Tina glared as she shoved her water bottle into her pack and stood. Big brothers, blood or not, could be so annoying.

TWO

Milo Bishop's fingers ached as he scooped snow from the drift. Ripping off his gloves, he shoved his freezing hands into his coat beneath his armpits and scowled at the pitiful excuse for a snow cave. He glared up at the mountain slope that had bucked him from his skis like a wild mustang and thrown him down the steep rocky side. That rock he had grazed as he had crested the peak had popped out of nowhere.

He growled, forced his hands into his gloves, and attacked the drift again with the piece of bark he used as a shovel. If his brother Jase had just come like he said he would for their annual Thanksgiving ski, Milo's mind wouldn't have been distracted. He would've enjoyed the day in the backcountry instead of wondering if he'd survive the night. He shifted his position to get a better angle at the drift and pain ratcheted up his leg, causing him to buckle to the snowy ground.

"Aaagh! Stupid knee!" He chucked the piece of bark into the drift. "Stupid mountain!"

He lay in the snow, his eyes closed to the pain throbbing in his knee and embarrassment thrumming through his blood. It wasn't his brother's fault that Milo wasn't paying attention. He should've known better than to come out alone. Heck, at the very least he should've replaced his pack when he'd busted the chest buckle instead of coming to the backcountry with broken gear. Then his pack wouldn't have wrenched from his back when he'd crashed, and his predicament wouldn't be so dire.

He tucked his hands under his arms and stared up at the clouds as they blew across the Colorado robin's egg colored sky in a fast clip. The trees towering above him had darkened, the sun closer to the western horizon than he liked. Dusk would come quickly in the gulch's bottom.

What had he been thinking? He'd been impulsive, giving in to the desire to be free to do whatever he wanted like his brother Jase did. He should've known being reckless would end badly for him.

Life only worked when he kept things under tight control, inhibiting his wants and emotions to do what needed to be done. He had lost his chance at off-the-cuff adventures when life had thrust him into manhood after his father's murder. His mom and brother depended on him. What would happen if he froze out here because of his rash stupidity?

The image of his mom collapsing in exhaustion from working two jobs again had him gritting his teeth. It had broken his heart to watch her become a shadow of who she'd been before the murder, working eighty plus hours at minimum wage jobs while he and Jase were in high school. It was why he'd joined the force instead of going to college. Well, that and the burning desire to keep lowlifes like the one who'd killed his father off the streets.

It pinched that Jase got the carefree life Milo had thought he had wanted, screwing around at college and doing whatever he felt like while Milo struggled to keep their family afloat and his emotions under wrap. He hadn't been able to brush off the weight of responsibility so easily. Hadn't wanted his mom to struggle when he could help. Now, thanks to his carelessness, he may have put his mom back where he'd worked so hard to pull her from.

He groaned as he rolled over, careful to keep his weight off his knee, and stared up the slope. Could he find some kind of crutch and make his way to wherever his fall had buried his pack? He shook his head. Putting weight on his leg would likely result in another tumble down the hill. Maybe crawling would be a better option?

A strong wind whipped through his coat with what sounded like his name floating on it. He scanned the area, as if someone else would be crazy enough to be out here in the middle of nowhere. Great. Not only was he stranded in the snow without a pack, but now he was hearing things.

He took one last fleeting look up the slope towards where he thought his pack might be, then turned back to digging out a shelter for the night. He doubted there was time to climb up to his gear and back down before darkness fell, so whatever measly shelter he could scrap from the snow would have to suffice.

He went back to digging, the grating noise and his

choppy breaths loud in his ears. He'd make it through the night. He might lose toes and fingers to frostbite, but he'd survive until someone showed up to rescue him.

Which would be better to lose, toes or fingers? He grimaced. Most women he knew would balk at a three-fingered man, but toes he could hide. Not that he had any desire for a relationship right now, anyway. He had to get Jase through college before he could even think about his next phase in life. He had it all planned out, though. Once Jase graduated, Milo could start looking for a wife.

His hands stung, and he shook them out. He'd probably be better staying a bachelor with his line of work. He never wanted to leave a wife struggling like his mom had had to.

He snorted. He hadn't had a date, let alone a girlfriend since his sophomore year in high school. Now he was contemplating marriage? The cold was messing with his mind.

The rush of feet dashing across the snow whipped him around to the next disaster in his misadventure. Freezing to death sounded better than being mauled and eaten. A large dog with a pack harnessed on its back careened towards Milo, its tongue hanging out the side of a mouth that appeared to be smiling. The beast landed on his chest, knocking him back into the snow. Its entire body wagged as it licked Milo repeatedly on the face.

He laughed at his futile attempt to push the dog off. "Okay. You found me."

How had search and rescue already been called out? They shouldn't have even worried until the next morning. Sure, he hadn't contacted his mom to check in like he said he would. Did she think so little of his abilities she had already sent out the cavalry? Milo pushed at the dog. How humiliating.

"Scout, for goodness sakes, let the man breathe." A woman's exasperated voice pulled both Milo and the dog's attention to the path the dog had come from.

Scout pushed off Milo's chest and careened towards the woman. The force snapped his head back against the snow, and a new pain exploded through his brain. Milo squeezed his eyes shut. Just great. Frozen fingers and an aching head. The crunching of snow and a plop beside him had him squinting one eye open against the throbbing ache.

"Milo."

His name puffed from the woman in obvious relief, filling the air with the scent of peppermint. Was she some kind of Christmas angel? Her blonde hair poked out of her stocking cap and framed cheeks pink with cold. She was small. If he could stand without buckling to the earth, she probably wouldn't even come up to his armpit. He peeked back the way she had traveled from, but the area was empty. What was this tiny, beautiful woman doing out here alone?

She tore her glove off with her teeth and slid her warm fingers down his cheek before taking his wrist and checking his pulse. Would she realize his pounding heart was because of her soft touch and not her dog's trample? Her light brown eyes held such worry he wondered if he was closer to dying than he thought.

"Milo, are you okay? Can you talk to me?" Her questions snapped him back to reality.

"Yeah. I'm fine." He groaned through gritted teeth, pushing himself up to sit.

Just great. Not only had he been an idiot going on this harebrained ski ill-equipped, but it appeared his embarrassment would be complete with a goddess rescuer. *That's it.* No more risky adventures. No more impulsive decisions. He peeked at the gorgeous woman next to him. It only resulted in trouble.

THREE

Milo Bishop. I'm rescuing Milo Hotstuff Bishop. Tina tried to calm her inner freak out as Milo sat up with a grimace. It didn't work. All the hopes of her freshman self being seen by the incredibly intriguing and completely gorgeous senior Milo Bishop bombarded her thoughts. How she'd sit by the front window of her foster home pretending to read when she knew Jase, her foster brother's best friend who happened to be Milo's younger brother, was coming over. If she glanced up at just the right time, she'd glimpse Milo when he dropped Jase off. Or how about all the times she'd hunkered at the small table in the school library during study hour, willing Milo to turn around from his study spot and notice her.

Wow. Had she really been that pathetic?

The memory of the one time he'd searched the shelves close to her table for a book came to mind. He had smiled and said hello, but the flash of perfect teeth and the sexy timbre of his voice had short-circuited her brain. Awe and mortification had merged as she had flapped her mouth like the rainbow trout her foster brother, Blake, liked to catch when they went to the river. Her face had erupted into volcanic temperatures, and Milo's lips had pinched like he tried hard to stifle a laugh. She'd stopped stalking him during study hour after that, preferring to hide in the far corner where the encyclopedias collected dust.

Now, here he was, still living up to her nickname for him, needing *her* to rescue *him*. Tina rolled her eyes as he glanced around. Who was she kidding? He had a decent snow cave going and could survive the night without her help. Hopefully, he wouldn't recognize her from school. Since she no longer wore the atrocious glasses that covered half her face, maybe she'd get away with him never making the connection. She just had to snap out of it and get to the whole rescuing the hero in distress part going.

"Are you out here by yourself?" Milo groaned and rubbed his knee, before turning his baby blues her way.

They were even more amazing up close.

"Yeah." Tina cleared her throat. "Scout and I are on an overnight training trip. When I called home to Stryker Security to check in, I was told you might be out here."

Tina shifted to his leg. Was it broken or just badly sprained? Before touching him, she glanced up at him in question and smiled.

"I'm Tina, by the way. Tina West."

"Milo, but I guess you already know that." Pain strained his voice.

"How's your knee?" She placed her palms on the sides of his leg to stabilize it.

"Twisted." Geesh, his scowl was even handsome. "I went one way as I tumbled down the hill, and my leg went the other."

"So, you don't think it's broken?" If it wasn't, she could work on getting hot food in him and setting up the tent.

"Nah. I think it's just sprained. Can't put pressure on it, though."

"Okay. That's good." She took off her pack and dug through it.

How much stuff did the guys add to her gear? Milo shoved his hands against his body and shivered. Right, fire first, then she'd work on shelter. Her face heated at the thought of her small, one-man tent and the sleeping bag they'd need to share. Maybe she should just call in the real rescue team and get them out of here.

She glanced at the sky. The horizon already showed the slight pinks of sunset. Unless Milo would die overnight, it would put the rescuers in danger if she called for an evacuation now. Looked like this training trip would be even more uncomfortable than she originally planned.

She pulled out her Bushbuddy stove and quickly set up the compact unit. With night coming on fast, it'd be best just to use the small stove to cook dinner and get settled in the tent. Rushing to the aspen trees, she broke off dry twigs from a downed tree to start the fire. Five minutes later, flames flicked around her titanium pot full of a freeze-dried stew and satisfaction flooded through her veins. Maybe she could do this whole search and rescue thing.

"Come and hold your hands over the fire." Tina scooted over to give Milo some space. "Do you have any gear?"

"Yeah." He motioned with his chin to the mountain. "Somewhere in the snow up there."

"Oh." Tina scanned the slope to see if she could find it. When she came up empty, she shrugged. "I have plenty to get us through the night. While we're waiting for the evac to arrive tomorrow morning, I'll see if Scout can locate your stuff."

"I'd appreciate it." Milo sighed as he held his hands close to the stove. "I'm kind of embarrassed I lost it. Should've replaced my pack when I noticed the broken strap."

Tina cringed. "That's a bummer."

He grunted. Tina turned away as she smirked. Living with Eva and her mother, Samantha, in their apartment at the ranch the last month had given Tina lots of experience with grumpy men. The angry slash of Milo's eyebrows, slumped curve of his shoulders, and the scornful sound of his voice told Tina he wasn't happy with himself. It shouldn't amuse her, but she couldn't help it. If he was anything like her friends, being saved by a woman probably pinched even more than needing to be rescued in the first place.

Well, if she wanted to prove to be deserving of that title, she needed to get busy. She yanked the way too small tent out of her pack and shook out the scant patch of fabric that had seemed larger the week before when she practiced setting it up. Laying it flat on the snow Milo had already packed down, she went to work popping the poles together. She tried to ignore the way he stared at her as she worked.

"Sorry, I'm useless right now." His voice pulled her eyes to where they already were fighting to go.

His cheek muscles clenched as he poked at the stew with her spork.

"You're not useless." She smiled to lift his spirits. "You're slaving over the stove."

He snorted, but the wrinkle in his forehead eased. Maybe if she got him talking, he'd ease up on himself.

"Do you go backcountry skiing often?" She threaded the pole into the tent's sleeve and moved to the next one.

"Not as often as I want to." He set the spork off to the side and looked at her. "My brother and I normally go on Thanksgiving day since our mom usually has to work. When he bugged out this morning, claiming he'd stayed up too late playing poker with the guys, I came on my own." He shook his head. "Guess I should've waited until later this weekend."

That sounded like Jase — always living for the minute, never following the rules. She couldn't remember how many times he and her brother had gotten in trouble for staying out too late. Blake's excuse had always been that the time had gotten away from them, but she had figured it was more likely they just hadn't cared. Why leave the life of the party when their foster parents never followed through on their punishments?

She glanced at Milo. Blake had often groused about Milo being hard on Jase, being a pain in the butt and acting all parental instead of enjoying life. Looked like nothing had changed in the Bishop family. A shame she couldn't say the same.

"That's family for you, always letting you down." Why did she say that? She stood abruptly. "I'm going to check in before I look at your knee and we get settled for the night."

She stomped to the middle of the clearing as she dialed the ranch. She'd have to watch what she said. Being around Milo might be her teenage self's dream come true. Forgetting what happened when you trusted the wrong people would be a nightmare she never wanted to repeat.

FOUR

Milo's hands shook uncontrollably as he watched Tina walk away. She intrigued him more than anyone had in a long time. Was she really a part of that security team holed up on the ranch outside of town? She had a sense of adventure, being out here in the backcountry all alone. If she was part of that team, she was capable. He scanned the gear she'd efficiently set up. All the latest stuff he'd been sticking in his wishlist but couldn't afford, at least not with Jase still in college.

She'd even pulled out items he'd never seen before, like the smoked sockeye chowder steaming a drool-inducing aroma to his brain. He'd have to check into this Heather's Choice company when he got home, maybe order a case of the stuff. If it tasted half as good as it smelled, he might decide to just live on chowder alone.

"Hey, Rafe." Tina's tired voice strained back to him. "I found Milo."

He scooted closer to the small fire, uncomfortable with the need to be found.

"Yeah, he's fine. Twisted his knee though, so we'll need an evac tomorrow morning." She peeked back at him, her eyes darting to the tent, then turned back around. "We'll be fine."

Why were her cheeks flushed with a blush? Milo's eyes snagged on the small shelter. Oh. He gulped. She hadn't planned on having company.

Maybe he should finish scooping out his snow cave. He shivered more violently at the thought of the freezing night ahead. He shook his head. It'd take hours to finish digging a shelter big enough. Scout whined and laid his head on Milo's leg.

"Yeah, probably not the smartest idea." He scratched behind the dog's ear. "Looks like we're in for a long, awkward night."

With them piled in her tent, they'd be plenty warm. Milo turned his attention back to Tina as she headed over. For being such a petite thing, she had gumption. They were deep in the wilderness, and she'd gotten there on snowshoes. Had she planned to come this far, or had she pushed because he'd gotten himself in a jam?

"You've got my location. See you in the morning." Tina smiled, a loud laugh escaping. "Whatever. Maybe you should stay out of trouble."

Her gaze connected with his, and she sobered. Ducking her head, she clicked off the call and stalked toward camp. How was she connected to Stryker Security?

They'd heard about the company down at the precinct. The owner of the security company had called officers out to take statements for an explosion that had happened out there. They came back with stories of super soldiers and a complex that rivaled Fort Knox. He had laughed it off as tall tales, just another rich guy throwing his money around. Now, though, she had piqued his interest.

"So, you're part of Stryker Security?" He studied her face as she kneeled by the stove.

Her lips twitched like she held in a laugh. "No, I'm just the nanny."

"What?"

He shook his head. Was he that cold? Because he thought she just said she was the nanny.

She smiled fully, her eyes sparkling with amusement. "I was hired as the nanny for Eva, the accountant's daughter. Samantha's ex's family was trying to kidnap Eva, so, since she can't go to preschool, they needed help keeping an eye on her."

The attempted kidnapping at the train depot came back to Milo. How could he have forgotten that Stryker Security had been involved with that situation?

"So, you have a background in private security?"

Tina snorted. "No. Waitressing."

Milo scrunched his forehead, rubbing his still-shaking hand over his neck. "I must be colder than I thought. My brain isn't working."

"Oh, shoot." Tina reached for the pot of soup. "Let me get you a cup of this. I'll also get you some ibuprofen."

She poured most of it into a tin cup she grabbed from her bag and handed it to him, then went to her first aid kit and grabbed a packet of painkillers. He wouldn't turn them down. He tried to lift the spork to his mouth, but his hand shook too much. He pinched his lips, frustration tightening his chest.

"Let me help." Tina scooted closer.

"No." Milo's voice came out harsh and short.

She flinched, the action twisting his stomach with regret. Here she was saving him, and he acted like a petulant child.

He sighed. "I'm sorry. I'm frustrated with myself, and it's making me grumpy."

"No, I get it." Tina swirled the remaining soup in the pot. "I'd be upset too."

"It's still no excuse to be a jerk."

Milo plopped the spork into her pot and lifted his cup to his lips. The creamy saltiness of the chowder soothed his nerves as it slid warmth to his stomach. He'd definitely be ordering a case when he got home.

"So, you're not a bodyguard?" Milo took another drink, gazing at her over the cup's rim.

She choked on a laugh, covering her mouth. "Oh, ouch." She closed her eyes. "Laughing with a mouth full of hot soup hurts." She rubbed her nose and shook her head. "I'm not a bodyguard. I had been working as a waitress while training to be a paramedic. Zeke, the owner of Stryker, had come to the coffee shop enough that we got to talking. Being ex-special forces, he'd been trained in emergency medical procedures and would ask what I was learning."

She shrugged, looking in her pot as she absentmindedly stirred the contents. What was bothering her? More importantly, why did he care? She sighed and took a bite.

"Anyway, he needed a nanny for Eva, and I needed a

better job." She smiled as Scout thumped his tail against the snow.

"If you're just the nanny, why are you out here?"

She stiffened. Could he be any ruder? He needed to shut his trap until his body returned to normal operating temperature and his brain started functioning properly.

"Well ... Zeke knows how I want to help others, so when Scout here retired from the military and needed a home, Zeke thought adding a K-9 unit to his services would be good." She reached over and ran Scout's ear between her fingers. "So, while I still help with Eva, Scout and I are training up. Well, I'm training. Scout already is amazing at this stuff."

Scout's entire body wagged as he moved from Milo's side to bury his head into Tina's lap. Instantly, Milo's warmth evaporated, and he missed the dog's heat. He shivered and took another drink, needing two hands to bring the cup to his mouth.

She looked up at the sky and took two quick bites. "The temp is just going to keep dropping. Let's get you settled and warmed in the tent. I don't want you getting any colder."

He nodded, too cold to talk. Warmth. Warmth would be good. His gaze darted to the small tent and back to Tina. Even the awkwardness of snuggling up to a stranger didn't bother him anymore.

FIVE

Tina rushed through the rest of her dinner, determined not to let the nerves of being in the small tent with her high school crush knot her stomach. Arranging the pad and sleeping bag as best as she could, she took a deep breath and turned to Milo. He sat by the stove, his head hung and shoulders slumped. His body shivered constantly despite having Scout's warmth curled back up against him.

"Come on, Milo. Let's get you warmed up." She went to his side to help him stand.

He held up his hand with a shake of his head. "I think it'll be easier if I just crawl over."

Tina rushed to the tent and turned open the sleeping bag. She winced as he grunted in pain and made his way to her, dragging his leg awkwardly behind him. Maybe she should take a closer look at his knee. He might need to get to a hospital quicker than in the morning. He flopped into the tent with his arm over his face and his chest heaving. She unclipped one of his ski boots and tucked it under the entry canopy.

"I'm so exhausted I'm not even embarrassed that I can't take off my own boots." Milo's muffled words made her grin.

"Well, you should be." She undid the other one. "Your feet stink."

He huffed a laugh, then groaned as he rolled all the way into the tent. She motioned Scout in and turned back to the stove. She cleaned up the pot and his cup with the pill packet trash sitting in the bottom, packed all the gear away but the first aid kit and compact lantern, and stowed everything in the tent's vestibule. Next, she took off her boots and tucked them under her gear. With the shelter meant for one person, there just wouldn't be space for Milo, Scout, her, and the gear.

She darted one last look around the almost dark forest, took a fortifying breath, and crawled into the tiny tent. As she zipped the tent closed, her heart raced faster and faster. *Stop being such a ninny.* She turned to find Milo staring at her.

"We should get out of our snow gear." Milo swallowed and pushed up to sit. "Packed in this tent like sardines, we'll hopefully get warm fast."

She nodded, already warmer than she should be. "Good. I want to inspect your knee."

"There's no use. It's an old injury. One I got chasing an escaped bull through the Glenwood Canyon." He smiled when she gasped, though it looked more like a grimace than a smile. "I'll tell you about it sometime."

"We aren't going anywhere anytime soon." She pulled off his coat and laid it along the edge of the tent.

He unbuttoned his snow pants and tried to shimmy them off his hips. "It's no use." He laid back with a grunt. "You're going to have to pull them off."

She shifted to his feet and willed the heat to cool from her cheeks. "How did a bull get loose in the canyon, and why were you chasing it down?"

She made quick work of getting his snow pants off, making sure to avert her eyes, though he wore thermalwear underneath. She wanted to be professional in this uncomfortable situation and ogling the way his shirt stretched tight across his muscular chest would be the exact opposite.

After piling his pants on top of his coat, she tucked her head and unzipped her own. Her hands shook with nerves. Geesh, it wasn't like she didn't hang out with hot guys all the time. Living at the ranch, she should be immune. Of course, the guys weren't her high school crush, falling into the older brother category.

She uncapped her canteen, took a chug, and extended it to Milo. He took a quick drink, then recapped it, his hands trembling. Her eyebrows pulled together. She could feel him shaking all over.

"Come on. We need to get you warm." She stripped off her snow pants, crawled into the sleeping bag next to him, and zipped it closed, glad the guys bought gear that was larger than the normal mummy bags.

She sucked in a yelp as he put his freezing feet on her calves. "Maybe I should rub those icy bricks and heat them up."

"No." He rolled onto his side and pulled her closer. "You're toasty."

Scout placed his head on Milo's shoulder with an exaggerated huff.

Milo chuckled, the sound vibrating against her palms pressed against his chest. "You're cozy too, Scout. Between the two of you, I'll heat up soon enough."

She relaxed her head against his bicep, the strain of staying rigid draining after the long trying day. There was no way she'd be able to sleep snuggled up to him like this. She hadn't been this close to another person since she and her foster sister, Faith, would sneak into each other's room and giggle under the covers late into the night.

Tina had been so confused and hurt when Faith said they shouldn't do that anymore. Tina now knew the insistence had come from Faith's fear their foster dad would turn on Tina as well. Maybe if Tina had pushed harder to keep the carefree escapades instead of sulking in her room upset, she could have helped Faith fight him off. Her heart ached in her chest. She couldn't think about that now.

Tina squeezed her eyes shut to the stinging tears and swallowed the lump in her throat. "Tell me about the bull."

She hoped he didn't catch the desperation in her tone. She hated that she needed a distraction, something to keep herself from spiraling into her past.

Milo's soundless laugh blew through her hair. "There was an accident in the canyon involving a semi full of ice cream and a trailer of rodeo bulls."

"No." She gasped, leaning her head back to look at his face in the lingering light.

His easy grin relaxed her as he spun a story about chasing cows through melting ice cream. She closed her eyes and pictured him slipping in Chunky Monkey while dodging an enraged bull, like some modern-day matador. Maybe if she kept him talking, her nightmares would stay tucked away.

SIX

Murmuring pulled Milo out of a deep sleep. Well, murmuring and the intense heat of being roasted alive. He took a deep breath and flexed his fingers. They were numb on one hand from the weight of Tina's head on his shoulder.

When she had first snuggled up to him, all he could think about was how glorious her warmth felt against his freezing body. He would've been stiff with unease like she had been, but the pain as his fingers and toes had warmed had him not caring how self-conscious the situation made him. As she had relaxed with his crazy stories, eventually falling to sleep with soft snores, he'd decided being rescued by the damsel wasn't such a horrible thing.

"No, no. Leave her alone." She whimpered and snuggled her face more into his neck.

Should he wake her up? While it wasn't pitch black in the tent, it couldn't be past six. A huff and lick in his ear had him pushing Scout away.

"Okay, okay." He whispered low to the dog, before turning his attention back to her. "Tina."

He placed his hand on her shoulder. She flinched, burying her face deeper into him. All his protective instincts flared to life, which was just plain dumb. She was having a nightmare, for goodness sakes, not facing a devouring dragon. Though from her quick breaths and the way she dug her fingers into his muscle, she probably was wrestling with monsters.

"Tina, wake up." He shook her harder, his voice loud in the quiet winter morning.

She screamed, shattering the calm of the wilderness and raising the hairs on his neck. She twisted and jerked to get away from him, kicking, punching, and scratching at his face. What in the world? Scout growled low and menacing behind Milo, the sound heightening the eeriness of the moment higher.

"Tina, wait. It's me, Milo ... Milo Bishop." He gritted his teeth as her leg connected with his knee.

She stilled, her breath chopping in between them. "Milo?"

He hated the smallness of her voice.

Hated the terror still lingering in her tone.

"Yeah, Tina, it's me." He rubbed his hand up and down her arm.

A sob wrenched from her before she jerked around and unzipped the sleeping bag. He sat up and clicked on the lantern that hung from the gear loft stretched across the top of the tent. She dashed her hand across her cheek before fumbling with the door.

"Tina, wait."

She didn't listen, just shoved her feet into her boots, yanked her coat from the pile in the corner, and dashed out into the chilly dawn. Scout darted after her, leaving Milo alone in the tent, wondering what the heck had just happened.

He scrubbed his hands over his face, willing his heart rate to slow back to normal. Talk about a confusing way to greet the morning. One part wondered if maybe getting serious about settling down wouldn't be a bad idea. Another worried he'd have his eyes gouged and his head mauled simultaneously.

He rubbed his chest where she'd hit him. She held quite a punch. He hadn't been hit that hard in a long time. Was that part of her training at Stryker or a skill she'd learned before?

He shook off the thought and reached for his snow gear. It was the bite of the morning that chilled him, not the memory of her words. Who was he kidding? Her terror would follow him through the day and maybe the night.

He had just maneuvered his pants over his hips when the crunch of her feet on the snow sounded outside. He scooted out of the way, giving her as much space as he could. His hands were sweating as he waited for her to come back in.

She huffed and pushed the door aside, sitting on the opposite side of the tent. "I'm sorry, Milo." Her voice held a tremor.

Was she embarrassed or still recovering?

"It's okay."

"You just ... startled me, I guess." She peeked up at

him from her twisting hands, before staring at the tent door.

"You want to talk about it?" Milo held his breath, wanting her to open up to him, not fully understanding the need to dive deep into what was running through her head.

"No."

Milo nodded, though his heart dropped into his stomach. The quick answer cut off all hope of finding out more about her. For now, at least. He shook his head at that thought. There was only now. The evac would show up, and they both would go on their merry way.

Did he want that? If the last two days had taught him anything, he should. If he wanted to pull his family from the pit they'd been thrown into with his father's death, he had to stick with the plan. Once Jase graduated, Milo could start thinking about his tomorrow. Until then, he had to keep his focus.

"When is the rescue crew arriving?" The sooner they got there, the better.

Tina glanced at her watch. "Not for another forty-five minutes or so." She forced a smile at him as she handed him a miniature candy cane. "Want me to help you get your boots on?"

"Yeah. Thanks." He popped the peppermint in his mouth, stashing the trash in his pocket.

She bent over his feet and helped push on his boots. He needed out of this space, out from her close presence that drew him like a bear to an open lunch pail. If he didn't get air, he might just pull her to him and give in to the impulse to kiss her pale pink lips. Rashness like that would derail him completely.

He hadn't had this much trouble focusing since his senior year when a cute freshman had distracted him during study hall. He smiled at the memory of those few months he had kept sitting at the same table day after day, inwardly yelling at himself to stop screwing around and do his work. It hadn't helped as he had found his gaze pulling again and again to the girl's table.

He had been too embarrassed to ask his friends who she was and too nervous to talk with her. When he'd finally said hello and she'd gone all red in the cheeks, he had thought maybe she was interested in him too. He had built up enough nerve to ask her on a date, but she had never shown up to the library again.

Tina tucked her hair behind her ear as she finished buckling his last boot. She resembled that freshman in a way. Maybe that was why he couldn't snap out of it. There was a slight possibility avoiding women hadn't been the best game plan after all. If he had gone on a date or two since high school, he wouldn't make such a fool of himself.

"You're all set." Her brown eyes held a sadness that her smile couldn't erase. "I'm going to go get breakfast ready. Let me know if you need help getting out."

"I can handle it." He swallowed hard.

She nodded and ducked out the door. He could breathe easier without her there. He snatched the sleeping bag pouch and shoved the bag in. He couldn't be a useless bum, making her clean up camp without him.

His brain and body had thawed now, so he could help her out.

Scout yipped, and Tina laughed. The sound opened up his tight chest, making it fuller than it had been in a long time. His hands stalled in their shoving. Nuts. Could she have thawed him too much?

SEVEN

Milo scowled as his brother Jase's face peered through the ER door window when the helicopter touched down at the hospital. The tension of the morning had eased as Milo and Tina had watched Scout search for his buried pack. Having his brother's smug face as the first thing Milo saw when landing reminded him why he'd been upset to begin with.

The helicopter jolted to a stop, and the rotors slowed as two nurses rushed to the door with a wheelchair. Tina held back as he maneuvered into the chair, a sweat breaking out on his forehead. He glanced back at the helicopter as the nurse wheeled him off. He waved Tina up next to him. He wanted to thank her before they got inside and whatever the doctors put him through started.

When she strode beside him with Scout on a leash, he cleared his throat, suddenly hesitant to say goodbye. "So, thanks for saving me."

She laughed and tucked her hair behind her ear. "You would've done fine without me."

"I would've lost toes, possibly fingers, and maybe been eaten alive without you." He reached for her hand, ignoring her flinch and giving it a squeeze. "Seriously, you and Scout are going to make a great S&R unit."

Her smile stretched across her face as she squeezed his hand in return. "Thanks, Milo."

The door to the hospital opened, and Jase sauntered out. "Tina? Tina West?"

Milo scowled as Tina yanked her hand from his.

"Hey, Jase." Her answer had all kinds of questions bubbling up Milo's throat.

"I can't believe it's you." Jase bounded out onto the landing pad and snatched her up into a hug, lifting her feet off the roof.

Scout's growl expressed Milo's thoughts perfectly. Tina held her body rigid, and her face turned a brilliant shade of red. If Jase didn't put her down, Milo was bound to jump from the wheelchair and knock the heavy thing over his brother's head. The thought of that brought more satisfaction than it should.

"Scout, no." Tina tapped Jase on the shoulder with one hand, while motioning to the dog with the other.

"You don't put her down, and that dog is going to go for your throat." Milo hoped Jase didn't catch the anger tinting his tone.

Jase wagged his eyebrows at Milo as he placed her down. "Man, Tina, it's been years."

Tina laughed as they moved into the hospital. "It's been three, Jase."

Three years? Did she know him from high school?

Milo shook his head. He would've remembered if she went to their school. She was unforgettable.

Jase waved off her retort. "So, are you the one who rescued my thickhead brother from certain death?"

Milo rolled his eyes as the nurse pushed him into an ER cubby. He lifted himself onto the bed, letting his legs hang over the edge while Tina shifted uncomfortably in the hall. Would she jet now that she'd gotten him here safely? Despite his brother's obnoxiousness, Milo hoped she stuck around for a bit.

"I didn't rescue him from anything." Tina crossed her arms. "I just happened to be in the same area."

Milo's head tingled, and he stifled a smile at her defense of him. Call it the pain from his leg or the annoying presence of Jase, but Milo couldn't hold the questions at bay anymore. Besides, he was a cop. That's what he did for a living.

"So, how do you two know each other?" He wasn't jealous, just inquisitive.

"You remember Blake Hunt, right?" Jase questioned.

Milo remembered that troublemaker best friend his brother had as teenagers. The two of them had made Milo worry he'd go pre-maturely gray or worse, bald. He nodded, hoping Jase didn't say Blake and Tina had dated.

"Tina is Blake's sister." Jase draped his arm over her shoulder. "She used to give us such a hard time for staying out late."

Milo's estimation of Tina rose even more. Then she flicked Jase's arm off her shoulder, and his esteem for her shot through the roof. So, no one had dated her—not that it mattered.

"Wait. Blake didn't have a sister. He was in foster care." Milo's words tumbled out before he thought.

Tina's body slumped, and her neck turned red. Shoot. He needed the doctor to check him out for foot-in-mouth disease. She peered down the hall toward the exit.

"Yeah, Blake and I were foster brats together." Tina's voice held an edge.

"I didn't mean ... that is, I didn't know Blake lived with other kids." Milo stumbled over his words as Jase looked on with glee, his eyes darting from Milo to Tina and back.

"Blake didn't want to be connected to the geeky girl with enormous glasses, especially when you still went to school with us." Relief washed over her face as she waved towards the entrance. "My ride's here."

Milo's mouth gaped open and shut as he tried to grapple with all that she'd just said. They went to school together? How did he not know her?

"Tina, wait." Jase winked at Milo before reaching for her arm. "Listen, we always go to the Hotel Colorado for the Christmas decoration lighting tonight. Why don't you join us?"

"Join you?" Tina's eyes widened.

"Yeah. It'd be great to catch up."

She glanced at Milo, and he leaned forward. He spoke before he could think of what to say.

"I'd like it if you came." He cleared his throat. Had he really just said that?

"You would?" Her voice squeaked.

"Yeah." He spoke though his mouth felt stuffed with cotton. "Yeah, I would."

"Okay." She blinked her eyes like she wasn't sure what had just happened.

He knew how that felt.

"Tasty Tina!" A man with too-perfect hair gave her a side hug.

Milo was getting sick of others hugging her. He clenched his fists next to his side, glad that he wasn't yet tucked into the bed like some invalid. Tina groaned, punching the man in the gut. Milo let his smirk free, not even bothering to hide it.

"Ugh, really? Like Tiny Tina wasn't bad enough?" Tina darted her eyes to him before turning back to her friend with a glare.

"What? Tasty Tina's a great name, and you know it. Glad the mountain lions didn't get a snack." The guy's smile proved he enjoyed razing people. "You going to introduce me to your friends?"

"No." Tina's deadpan answer caused Milo to snort.

"I'm wounded. Right here." The man placed his hand over his heart before extending it to Jase. "Rafe Malone, self-appointed big brother, computer genius, and overall awesome extraordinaire."

"More like Rafe Malone, perpetual gamer and slacker extraordinaire," Tina quipped under her breath.

"Jase Bishop." Jase shook Rafe's hand, seemingly finding enjoyment in someone else who liked to joke around.

"You must be Milo." Rafe extended his hand to Milo.

"That's me." He gripped tighter than necessary.

"Glad our Tina found you." Rafe leaned in,

squeezing harder. "You didn't take advantage of the situation, did you?"

Tina gasped and smacked Rafe on the back. He laughed, stepping back beside her, though a glint of seriousness held in his eyes. He may act like a jokester, but this Rafe held substance. Milo would have to remember that.

"Hey! Isn't that what big brothers are supposed to ask?" Rafe held his hands up in surrender.

"You are not my brother." Tina grabbed his arm and pushed him toward the exit. "And we are leaving before you embarrass me even more."

"You're no fun." Rafe waved. "Nice to meet you both."

Tina smiled and headed down the hall.

"Tina?" Why couldn't Milo just let her go?

She peeked back, her eyebrows rising. "Yeah?"

"Meet you at the parking lot across from the Brewpub at seven?"

She bit her lip, tucking her hair behind her ear. "Sure."

Warmth spread through his chest as she left. His mouth lifted on one side in a smile as he pushed back to lie down. He shouldn't be so pleased that she was coming with them tonight. Really, he shouldn't, especially since it went completely against his plans. Besides, she was just meeting up with them as friends, a chance to catch up with Jase. No matter what he told himself, he couldn't wait to see her again.

"Oh, man. You and Tina West?" Jase grinned like a cat that had swallowed a mouse. "That's dope, bro."

"Dope? What are you, like twelve?" Milo shook his head. "There's nothing there."

"Yeah, right," Jase scoffed as he plopped in the chair, motioning wide with his hands. "Like there wasn't electric tension zinging between you two." Jase held up his phone and snapped a picture of Milo. "This is going up on Facebook. The tough Milo Bishop, rescued by a pixie."

"Don't you dare." Milo reached for Jase's phone, but he tucked it in his pocket.

"You know, you two would be good for each other." Jase couldn't possibly get more annoying. "You're a stick in the mud, never drawing out of the lines. She's quiet as a mouse, always following the rules. Match made in heaven."

Milo's heart pounded in his chest like those silly cartoons they had watched as kids.

"Whatever. Make yourself useful and go get me some coffee."

Jase hopped up and saluted, for once listening to what Milo said. Jase paused at the door, looking down the hall before turning back to Milo.

"Just ... if you think nothing's there, don't string her along." Jase hit his fist against his thigh. "She's already been through enough for three lifetimes."

Milo pushed himself up in the bed. "What does that mean?"

"That's her story to tell." Jase shook his head. "I'm just here to fetch the coffee."

He disappeared down the hall, leaving Milo sputtering to himself. Tina's nightmare earlier rushed back to his thoughts, chilling him like he was back on the mountain. Just what had happened to her?

EIGHT

"What was I thinking?" Tina muttered to herself as she chewed the last of her candy cane.

Scout whined in his crate as Tina drove down Blake Avenue. Why had she agreed to meet Milo and his family? Seriously?

She shook her head. She knew why. When Milo had told her what time with a look of expectation on his face, her inner teenage self jumped up and down in squealing glee.

The rest of the day, her rational adult brain kicked in, leaving her with a knotted stomach and heartburn. She could just not show up. She could take a left on Eighth and meet the others where they were parking at Summit Canyon Mountaineering.

"Dolt. What if you run into the Bishops?" She scowled, and Scout yipped in the back. "We could just go home?"

The dog whined like that was the worst idea ever. Tina had to agree. She'd had a lingering edge of fear skittering under her skin all day long. The unfortunate result of the morning's nightmare left her wanting distraction, not cavernous silence.

She passed Eighth Avenue, taking one longing look down the street, then continued toward the river. Her hands slicked the steering wheel with sweat as she slowed and pulled into the parking lot. Milo leaned against the passenger side of an older model Subaru Forester typical of the area while Jase spoke with a woman in her early fifties on the sidewalk.

Tina's heart pounded in her throat as Milo's gaze followed her into the empty spot beside him. He looked amazing. She knew time had been good to him after last night, but seeing him all spiffed up in a leather jacket that hung just right, his wavy brown hair falling perfectly, and a five o'clock shadow darkening his jaw made her throat go impossibly dry.

She had fantasized about running her fingers through his hair as a teenager. Good to know she had changed little in the last six years. She threw the car into park as she rolled her eyes. She needed to get a grip. She was here because Jase wanted a trip down Memory Lane, though she didn't remember many memories she'd consider wonderful from high school.

Milo scanned her car from the hood to the hatch, his one eyebrow lifting in question, and her face heated. Why had she let Zeke buy her this car? Sure, he'd felt terrible her old one had blown up, but, really? Did he have to pick an Audi? At the time, she'd been thrilled for something reliable. Now, she wished she had insisted on something that fit her better, something beat-up and just clunking along.

Milo opened her door, and she climbed out. "Hey." He scanned her quickly like he had the car and swallowed.

She tried not to fidget, instead pointed to the brace on his knee. "How's the leg?"

"Just pulled. Doc wants me to keep the brace on for a week. Keep off of it if I can." He shrugged and rubbed his thigh.

"I don't think you're following the doctor's orders." Tina huffed a laugh and headed to the hatch to let Scout out. "You should've just called and let me know you couldn't come."

"I'll be fine." He limped beside her. "Besides, I didn't want to miss seeing yo—the lights." He ran his hand across his neck and glanced towards the river.

Heat spread up her chest and into her face. Was he about to say you? A low whistle came from behind Milo.

"An Audi A4?" Jase strode up with a woman who looked like a delicate version of Milo. "This is the newest model, even. If this is the kind of vehicle a nanny can afford, sign me up."

Her face went from the enjoyable flush of Milo's almost slip to the hot-as-Hades burning of embarrassment. She was glad for the dim lighting of the parking lot because she was positive her face flamed from chin to hairline. Curse her fair skin, and curse Zeke for being a gazillionaire.

"I can't actually afford this. My boss bought it for me

out of guilt." Tina stuttered as she reached for Scout's kennel.

"Why did he feel guilty?" Milo's arms crossed his chest and his brow wrinkled.

Nuts. He could take that all kinds of ways. Most of them not good.

"Nothing bad, really." She clipped Scout's leash on. "These guys, terrorists, tried to get one of Zeke's clients and strapped a bomb to my car to force his hand."

Mrs. Bishop gasped as Scout jumped from the car. The dog could be intimidating to some, so Tina snapped her fingers in command. When Scout sat at her side, she looked up to find all three of the Bishops gaping at her. She tucked her hair behind her ear.

"Everything okay?" She clicked the button to close the hatch and slid the keys into her jeans.

"You had a bomb strapped to your car?" Milo's words came out low and harsh through gritted teeth.

"Well, it wasn't strapped. I think they just stuck it on." She shrugged, glancing over his shoulder towards the train depot. They'd miss the lighting if they didn't get going. "I didn't get to see it."

"Oh, my." Mrs. Bishop's hand fluttered against her chest. "Is this a regular occurrence where you work?"

"No ... though June set off a makeshift explosion in her house, but that happened in Tennessee." Tina's admiration of June had rocketed when they'd heard the story from Cooper. "I'm Tina. You must be Mrs. Bishop."

"Call me Maggie, dear." She had a kind smile, like one of those moms that greeted the kids at the door with a hug and a cookie.

Her foster mom, Susan, had been like that. She'd always been so happy to see Tina. She needed to swing by to visit her soon.

"That's it." Jase put his hands in his pockets and smiled wide. "I'm becoming a Manny. Do you need an assistant, Tina?"

She laughed. "No. Though if people keep getting lost in the woods, I might."

She grinned up at Milo, but his serious expression had her biting her lip to contain it. She needed to move this party along, get them off the topic of Stryker before she ruined the evening. Could Zeke get in trouble for what had happened? She frowned. No, the cops had come out and talked with them. Of course, that had been the next day after she got back from playing the decoy for June and Sosimo's escape. Maybe she should just keep quiet about ranch business.

NINE

"Why don't we make our way over the bridge?" Mom forced a smile and threaded her arm through Jase's, pulling him towards the street.

Milo limped alongside Tina. Pain shot up his leg with each step. He gritted his teeth to keep from groaning. Maybe he should just go home, put up his foot, and find a game to watch.

He glanced at Tina. She was such a juxtaposition. She was small, her pretty face sweet and innocent, like a preschool teacher. Or a nanny. But she hiked through the backcountry with only her dog and talked about not being able to see the bomb strapped to her car with obvious regret.

His urge was to protect her, but she didn't need protecting. Heck, she'd saved him. He was in uncharted territory, and he didn't know how to proceed—or if he even should.

The smell of fried food filled the air as they passed the Brewpub. Maybe he could talk her into grabbing something to eat before the evening ended. He could go for some chicken nachos or fish and chips.

"I talked to the guys that went out to take the report." Milo shoved his hands in his coat pockets to keep from grabbing her elbow as they crossed the street. "Actually, they talked to everyone who would listen about the explosion. Pretty nasty business."

"Yeah." Tina shrugged. "I won't lie. It was scary. The worst part was getting up the nerve to jump out of the car, not knowing if it'd blow up before I reached Rafe's arms."

He stumbled, his stomach bottoming out. She glanced at his knee and slowed down. He'd let her think it was his injury that tripped him up and not the proverbial bucket of ice dumped on his head.

"Before I could even sigh in relief at being alive, Rafe had scooped me up like a baby and ran into the house." She chuckled...chuckled!

His throat felt like a Christmas ornament had been shoved down it. She was unlike any woman he'd ever met. Daring ... dangerous. A breeze blew as they crossed the bridge to the other side of the Colorado River, and she pulled her collar up around her neck.

"So, you guys come for the lighting every year?" She peeked at him as she reached down and gave Scout a quick pat.

"Yeah. My parents had come here for their first date, so every year they'd drag us down."

Now, why'd he say that? Would she think he thought this was a date? He peeked at her. Was it? No, if this was a date, he sure as shooting wouldn't have his mom and brother tagging along.

"That's so sweet." She bit her lip, turning her attention to the opposite side of the bridge. "I bet it means the world to your mom that you still come down here with her."

"I guess so."

That year after his father had died, it had surprised him Mom had wanted to still come. She'd spent the night wiping tears from her cheeks, but the smile had been the first real one he'd seen in months. That day he'd sworn he'd make sure they came every year, no matter what.

Jase and Mom stopped at their usual spot and leaned against the railing. Mom placed her head on Jase's shoulder, squeezing his arm in a hug. Milo was glad he could help her so she didn't have to work so hard. Was happy her skin no longer hung on her bones and her eyes weren't bruised with exhaustion.

She smiled at him and Tina, as they approached. "Tina, honey, we usually stand back here, rather than venturing closer. I like to see the hotel as a whole, before exploring all the details."

"That sounds great." Tina gazed at the historic building. "I've never seen the Christmas lights. I mean, I've seen them as I've driven past but have never spent the time really looking."

She tucked her hair behind her ear in what Milo now recognized as a nervous habit. Her expressive brown eyes took in the crowd with caution. Jase's comment at the hospital replayed for the millionth time that day. Just what had her childhood been like?

"How long have you lived in Glenwood?" His mom snuggled closer to Jase as another crisp gust blew off the river.

"I've lived in the Roaring Fork area my whole life." Tina glanced behind her like maybe she wanted to escape back to her car.

"And you've never seen the Hotel Colorado lights?" His mom was gearing up for her typical exasperation when she learned about locals not knowing Colorado history.

"Nope. Just always drove right by."

Mom tsked. "Parents these days. Not taking their kids to a historic icon. Why, Teddy Roosevelt used to stay at this hotel when he'd come to Colorado to hunt. The halls on the main floor alone are brimming with so many stories of our past."

"Mom, geesh. Lay off the sermonizing." Jase bumped Mom with his shoulder. "Tina was in the foster system with Blake, remember."

Tina shifted her feet back and forth, obviously uncomfortable. Milo wanted to deck Jase. Did his brother have to be such an insensitive dolt?

"Oh, dear. I'm sorry." Mom's eyes darted from Milo to Tina before she reached for Tina's hands that clenched Scout's leash. "Please forgive me. I get kind of crazed when it comes to history. I always thought it'd be fascinating to be a historian and never understand that others aren't as passionate about it as I am."

"It's okay." Tina's smile looked forced.

Mom bent down to Scout. "And this must be the

amazing search dog." She rubbed behind his ears. "Thank you for helping find my lost lamb."

"Mom." Milo groaned. "Lamb? Really?"

"Milo, even though you are six feet tall and have taken care of this family for almost half your life, that doesn't mean you're not still my lamb." Her serious tone contradicted her jovial expression as she gave Scout one last pet before standing.

He peeked at Tina. Her lips were pressed flat together like she held in a laugh. Well, he'd take the embarrassment if it eased hers.

"Mom, if you're going to call a man an animal, you need to pick one more masculine, like a ram or mountain lion." Jase dropped his arm across her shoulders.

"If you want me to call you kitten, I can do that, honey." She patted him on the chest, a smug look upon her face.

Jase sputtered as Tina burst out laughing. Milo snorted, thrilled his brother was getting a taste of his usual joking manner. Scout barked, pressing his head into Mom's hand. She glanced at her watch, her face brightening in excitement.

"Now, hush. The lights are about to come on." She wrapped her arm around Jase's waist.

"Because we have to keep quiet for our eyes to work." Jase grumbled.

Tina smiled up at Milo, her face bright with amusement. Milo's heart thumped in his chest like he'd just had a run in with another crazed bull. He'd have to think about thanking Jase for meddling later.

Milo inched closer to Tina so their arms grazed each other. "You ready for the show?"

"Bring on the lights." Millions of colors flashed on like it had been her command that flipped the switch.

She gasped, her mouth dropping wide in amazement. Milo couldn't help but stare at her as her eyes darted this way and that to take it all in. She was more captivating than a bunch of lights.

"Suzie!" A man's yell lifted above the crowd, pulling Milo's attention from Tina. "Suzie!"

A woman's frantic calls followed the man's, and Milo pushed through the crowd towards the commotion, wincing with each step. A pregnant woman surrounded by three children darted around the people in the crowd, searching frantically. Her face was contorted in anguish. A man, who Milo assumed was her husband, stood on a bench and scanned the area, yelling.

"Ma'am, Glenwood PD, how can I help?" Milo touched her elbow to get her attention.

"My daughter's missing." The woman sobbed. "She was just here, skipping around the bridge."

"What does your daughter look like? What's she wearing?" Milo shot off the questions as people gathered around.

"She's four years old. She has curly blonde hair and is wearing a bright teal peacoat." The woman covered her mouth with one hand and wrapped her belly with the other. "Oh, God, help us. What if she's stolen? What if we never find her?"

Her husband rushed up, whipping his hat off of his head. "I can't see her."

"Do you have anything of hers in your purse? Anything she has worn or a toy she handles often?" Tina pushed up closer to Milo.

How had he forgotten about Scout? Milo nodded at Tina. She could find the child. Not a lot of time had passed for the girl to get very far.

"Yes." The girl's mother shoved her hand in her pocket and pulled out a pair of mittens. "Will this work? She wouldn't keep them on. Kept dropping them on the ground."

Tina grabbed the mittens. "These are perfect." She bent down to Scout and held the items up to him. "Okay, buddy. You ready to go to work?"

The dog's tail wagged as he nosed the mitten. He sniffed it all over while Tina patiently waited. He looked up at Tina with what Milo would call a nod.

"Go find her." Tina motioned with her hand, and Scout's nose hit the ground.

He sniffed low, then lifted his head in the air. With a bark, he rushed back over the bridge in the direction they'd just come from. Milo hobbled as fast as he could behind them.

Scout slowed where the bridge led to the road, zigzagging back and forth on the platform. When the parents and the crowd pressed in close, Milo put his arms out and turned around.

"Folks, stay back. Let the dog work." He raised his voice above the excitement, glancing at Jase for help.

"Please, calm down. We need to help the handler by not being a distraction for the dog." Jase's tone held authority and reason most newbie cops couldn't even pull off. His face was, for once, lacking its typical humor.

Milo turned to his mom. "Call this in. Get back up over here."

She nodded and moved away from the crowd as she pulled her phone out of her pocket. Milo glanced at Scout just as the dog sniffed the mitten again and dashed down the stairs, heading west. Tina held the leash lightly in her hand, watching intently as her dog canvased his way down the sidewalk. He stopped at a vacant parking spot along the street, his nose working this way and that along the ground and in the air.

Traffic rushed up and down the busy road, leaving Milo with a sinking feeling in his gut. His gaze kept skipping from Tina to Scout, hoping for an encouraging sign but knowing one wouldn't be coming. He hated knowing that, statistically, the search would come to nothing. The knowledge didn't keep the frustration banked when Scout lowered himself to his belly on the sidewalk with a whine, and Tina's shoulders slumped.

Didn't keep the anger at bay at the creep who would steal a child away from their family.

Anger at himself for being so distracted.

Tina bent down to Scout, rewarding him with enthusiastic pats and pulling a toy out of her purse. What must she be feeling, having to act happy for her dog, knowing they hadn't been fast enough to find the child? He pushed the question aside and turned to the distraught parents. He had a job to do, one that needed his complete focus if he had any chance of finding this girl.

TEN

"I'M so thankful you're able to join us for dinner." Mom stirred her Palisade peach pie filling on the stove, the smell of cinnamon and sweet fruit competing against the turkey roasting in the oven.

Milo's mom had set him to work peeling and cutting vegetables for the tray the minute he'd hung his coat in the hall. Every year she made enough for a crowd of people, even though there were just the three of them, and every year he and Jase pitched in. The last few Thanksgivings were some of the few guaranteed times they'd all be together. Like normal, Jase was shirking his job, the shower running upstairs though it was well after noon.

"Yeah, well, there's not a lot we can do on the case at the moment." He slid the knife through the celery with extra force.

"Could you not get anything off of the surveillance cameras?" She worked the pie crust onto her rolling pin and eased it into the pan.

"No. I've gone through all the video feed following the guy all the way up the valley toward Aspen and lost him." Milo tossed the celery in the section of the tray. "Do you know how many Subaru Outbacks there are in this county?"

"Um..."

"Thousands. There was at least ten the same sage color that traveled the highway within the hour of the kidnapping."

"And you couldn't run the plates?"

"No, something obstructed them, probably on purpose." Milo sighed. "We've pulled up registration information on that make and model and have officers questioning owners. It'll take a long time to go through all of them, though."

"Those poor parents. That poor little girl." Mom sniffed as she poured the pie filling into the crust. "And to think we were right there."

"That's the frustrating thing." Milo snatched up a carrot and attacked it with a peeler. "If we had been two minutes earlier, two minutes, Scout and Tina would've found them easily."

"Those two were incredible to watch." Mom carefully arranged the top crust on the pie.

"Yeah, they're incredible."

Milo thought about how beautiful Tina had looked the morning after she'd found him. Her stocking cap pulled low over her ears. No make-up. Her eyes bright with excitement as they had watched Scout find Milo's buried pack. Man, how he wished he could've seen excitement rather than disappointment in her eyes the night before.

"Milo, honey, when are you going to give Tina a call?" Mom pinched the edge of the peach pie like she hadn't just thrown a bomb into the middle of their conversation.

"Um ... I hadn't thought about it." Lie, but she didn't need to know that. He peeled the carrot without seeing it.

"Milo Jacob Bishop, don't lie to your mother." She stared him down over the kitchen island.

He held her gaze, though a bead of sweat dripped down his back. His mom hadn't scolded him in years. Granted, he hadn't done anything to warrant it in the past, especially after his dad had died. Truth was, she wasn't much of a scolder, even when he and Jase deserved it.

"What's he lying about, Mom?" Jase had to pick that moment to decide to help.

"He's trying to convince me he doesn't want to call Tina and ask her out on an actual date," Mom answered as she cut slits into the pie top.

Milo groaned internally. Did they have to be having this conversation right now?

"What's the problem, bro? You like her don't you?" Jase snagged a celery stick and snapped into it with his teeth.

"You sound like you're in high school." Milo tossed the mutilated carrot into the tray and grabbed another.

"You sound like you're scared." Mom put her fists on her hips.

"Ooh, those are fighting words." Jase grinned at Mom

before turning to Milo. "So, she scares you, huh? It's because she's tough and might have more nerve than you, right?" Jase nodded as Milo scowled at him. "I get it. I mean, did you catch how she seemed upset about not getting to inspect the bomb under her car? That level of guts in a girl would intimidate most men."

"I'm not intimidated." Not much, at least. "It's just not a good time right now."

"Why not?" Mom crossed her arms over her kiss-the-cook apron, determination flaring from her eyes.

"Work is nuts right now." Milo focused hard on the carrot, running the peeler over it with deliberate slow strokes.

"Lame." Jase snagged another celery.

"That's hogwash." Mom slapped her palms on the counter. "You have days off. Your evenings are free most of the time. We live in Glenwood Springs, for Pete's sake, not Denver."

"Glenwood has crime," Milo countered weakly.

It did, more than he liked, but they didn't live in a city. In fact, there was just one other detective and their supervisor, Detective Jeff Stone, in the investigations department with Milo. While they stayed busy and could use another person on the team, they weren't drowning in work.

"Why isn't it a good time?" Mom pushed.

"Besides being busy at work? Jase is still in school, and I'm still a year away from having this house paid off." Milo tried to keep the frustration out of his voice, but they really had no clue.

Jase's lips pressed together as he stared at the celery in

his hand. Mom let out a heavy sigh, leaning into her hands still braced on the counter. He didn't want to ruin Thanksgiving more than it already had been, but the pained expression on his mom's face told him he was doing just that.

"Can we just drop it ... please?" Milo grabbed another carrot, praying they'd listen.

"Honey, I've been afraid of this." Mom's voice had lost some of its power. "I should've said something earlier. Should've never let it happen, but I was just selfish."

"What are you talking about?" Did he want to know?

"It's not your job to provide for us, Milo. Not anymore. Never should've been in the first place." Mom's shoulders slumped. "After your father died, I was so overwhelmed, I wasn't sure what to do. I let you step in and do more than any young man should have to."

"I didn't mind, Mom. You needed the help."

"You're right. At first I did." She sighed and rubbed her fingers over her collarbone. "But ... I was wrong to rely on you for so long and allow you to think you had to push your dreams aside to take care of us."

Mom motioned between her and Jase. Jase leaned back against the other counter, a flat look on his face. It surprised Milo that Jase wasn't putting his two cents in. Wasn't saying some smart alec remark about Milo being too bossy.

"I haven't put my dreams aside."

"When was the last time you went on a date?" His mom's question pinched.

"I've dated."

"When?"

"Sophomore year." Jase muttered low. "The last time you went on a date was your sophomore year in high school."

How could he possibly know that? Milo's neck and ears heated. He gripped the peeler and carrot hard in his palms.

Mom huffed a humorless laugh. "I've been on more dates than you." She shook her head. "Do you know how horrible that makes me feel?"

Man, she was full of bombs today.

"You've dated?" He couldn't keep the shock from his voice.

"Yes, I've been dating. In fact, Jeff is joining us for dinner."

"That's great, Mom." Jase smiled, seeming to snap out of his mood.

"Jeff, who? Why didn't you tell me?" Milo hated that he'd missed something so important.

"Well ... um ... we wanted to keep things quiet until we decided if we even liked each other." She cleared her throat.

"Who is this guy?" Milo narrowed his eyes.

Could he run down to the station before dinner and do a background check? Her cheeks turned a stunning shade of pink. He couldn't remember ever seeing his mom blush.

"Well, he's..." Mom swallowed, her gaze dashing to Jase before it came back to Milo. "I ... that is, Jeff Stone and I've been dating."

The peeler and carrot clattered to the cutting board.

Milo blinked, not sure if he'd heard her right. He shook his head.

"Jeff Stone, as in Detective Jeff Stone ... my boss?" Milo took a step back from the counter. "But he's younger than you."

Her eyes narrowed to slits. "Not by much."

She was only about five years older than Jeff. He looked around the room, trying to find something to ground himself with. How could his mom be moving on? How could she take the next step in life when he hadn't even taken the first? He wanted to be happy for her. He did ... he was. He'd never wanted her to wallow in grief for his dad. But the fact that she might not need him anymore, might have never needed him, left a cavernous feeling in the base of his stomach.

"That's not what we're talking about, anyway." Mom closed her eyes and took a deep breath. She opened her eyes, and Milo steeled himself for what she would say. "Milo, I've been wrong in leaning on you too much."

"Mom—"

She held up her hand. "It's true. God knows I appreciate all that you've done for this family, but it's well past time that you start living for yourself. You need to stop taking care of us, Milo, because, believe it or not, Jase and I are capable of taking care of ourselves."

"But—"

"You don't have to worry about Jase's schooling. That's for me and him to mess with." Her voice was gaining strength again. "You don't have to worry about my house payment. I make enough to cover it. In fact, I didn't even know you were paying the mortgage down." She chuckled. "Guess I should look at the bills better."

"Mom, I don't mind."

"But I do." She circled the island and put her hands on his cheeks. "Milo, I want more for you than just work and us. I want you to find adventure with someone special, like I did with your dad." Her smile was bittersweet. "I saw how you looked at Tina, hun. Don't think I didn't notice the chemistry bouncing between you two."

"It's pretty zingy, huh?" Jase chuckled from his spot against the counter.

"Oh, yeah." Mom chuckled. "When was the last time you noticed a woman like that?"

"I don't know." His voice cracked.

"Don't you think it's worth seeing if something is there?" She patted his cheek. "I do."

"Okay." He swallowed the boulder in his throat. "I'll call her."

Mom pulled him in for a hug. He buried his face into her neck, breathing in the comforting smell of cinnamon and peaches that clung to her. Could he just let go of the responsibilities like she said? It had been his focus for so long. He doubted he could. She squeezed him tighter and patted his back.

"I've been so blessed by you, honey. More than you'll ever know." She whispered in his ear, "I hear the winter concerts at the fairy caves can be quite romantic."

She pulled back, patted him on the shoulder, and turned to Jase. "You're on veggie duty. Your brother has a phone call to make."

Jase crowded up to Milo's spot at the counter,

pushing him out of the way with a snicker. "You said doody."

"You're such a child." Mom rolled her eyes.

They went to work on the meal as Milo backed from the room. Could he take the chance and call Tina? He wanted to, wanted to a lot. He glanced at his mom as she smiled at something Jase said. Well, if she could start dating, maybe it was past time for him to as well. He wiped his slick palms against his pants as he strode out onto the porch, pulling his phone from his pocket. *Here goes nothing.*

ELEVEN

Tina's knee bounced as she sat on the island's stool in the main ranch house waiting for Milo to pick her up. Her stomach twisted like the knotted yarn Eva had tried to "fix" earlier while they did crafts. Her insides had been twisting all week since agreeing to go out on an actual date with Milo.

She glanced around the busy living room, her friends lounging, waiting to pounce on the poor guy. Why hadn't she told Milo to come to her apartment? Now, the embarrassment of him pulling up to the garage she lived above with Samantha and Eva didn't seem half as bad as him having to go through the gauntlet of all the team.

Would the guys behave? They yelled at the screen in unison as they played some Mario Kart racing game on the console. She sighed. Doubtful.

"Haha, losers!" Rafe gloated, doing a victory dance in the living room and high fiving a less enthusiastic Jake.

"Uncle Rafe, you're being a stinky winner." Eva sat up straight from where she leaned into her mom, her adorable face scrunched in disappointment. "You're supposed to be nice when you win, otherwise no one will want to play with you anymore."

"We don't want to play with him now." Derrick grumbled where he slumped, dejected on the floor in front of her, his long legs stretched out into the middle of the room.

Eva climbed over Derrick's shoulder from the couch and sat on his lap. The tough black man grunted as she kneed him in the head. Concern shone in her blue eyes as she placed her tiny hands on both of Derrick's cheeks. Tina leaned in closer so she wouldn't miss what Eva said. She always came up with some doozies that would keep Tina laughing for hours.

"Uncle D, I promise I won't be a stinky winner when I beat you to a pulp." Eva's serious tone had everyone sputtering with laughter.

"Eva!" Sam gasped and pushed off of where she leaned into Zeke on the couch.

"What?" Eva's eyes were wide in confusion. "He's not a good player."

The room erupted into laughter, and Tina's stomach unraveled a little. While she still worried about what the guys would say to Milo, she was glad she wasn't twisting her hands alone at the apartment. Scout whined and moved to Derrick, placing his head on Derrick's lap like he felt sorry for him.

"Oh, man. Even the dog thinks I'm pathetic." Derrick chuckled as he petted Scout behind the ears.

The laughter doubled, and Tina's face hurt from smiling. Lights flashed across the yard. What? How'd

Milo get through the gate? The ball of yarn in her gut turned into a snake and slithered up her throat. She was supposed to have the time from when he buzzed at the gate to the drive to the house to calm herself.

"How'd he get through?" Her voice squeaked out.

Rafe smirked. "I opened the gate about ten minutes ago. Figured he shouldn't have to wait to pick you up. That might have made him nervous."

Rafe worried about Milo being nervous? What about her nerves? She stood from the stool, her eyes glued to the door. She should just walk over there and meet him outside. It'd be so much easier and less embarrassing than having him meet everyone.

"Hold on, Tasty." Rafe held up a hand and motioned for her to sit. "We have to interrogate ... I mean, meet him, before we let him take our Tina out."

She glared at him, her arms crossing over her chest. That nickname had to go. She hadn't been mountain lion lunch, far from it. Besides, someone might get the wrong idea.

Rafe snapped the door open, a scowl on his face like he really was getting ready to interrogate Milo. *Note to self*. Next time she had a date, they were meeting wherever it was they were going. No more coming to the ranch.

Milo entered through the door, his eyes scanning the crowd before landing on Tina. Did his lips turn up at the corners when he saw her, or was that just wishful thinking? How could someone look so handsome in a leather coat and jeans? Seriously? No one should be able to be that good looking.

He stretched out his hand to Rafe, earning points for upfront bravery. "Rafe, nice to see you again."

Rafe's eyebrows rose a fraction before he uncrossed his arms and shook Milo's outstretched hand. "You, too. Looks like you're all healed up."

Milo nodded and shrugged one shoulder. "Yeah. The knee still aches, but I'm free of the brace."

"Come on in." Rafe motioned towards the living room. "Let me introduce you to everyone."

Tina crossed the room, trying not to sprint. How could she get Milo out of the house without being rude? Why'd her brain have to draw a blank now?

"We've got to hustle if we want to make it to the caverns on time." Tina snatched her purse from the table.

Milo's mouth lifted on one side. "It's all right. We've got time."

Tina inwardly groaned as she sidled up beside him. She turned to the room and pointed as she rattled off names. Samantha bit her lip in obvious amusement next to Zeke, whose eyebrows were low over slitted lids. Kiki toed Jake on the other side of the couch and wiggled her eyebrows up and down. Jake shrugged back. This was all too much.

Eva crawled off of Derrick's lap and rushed over. Oh, no. Tina found Eva endearing, but she worried what the imaginative girl would say.

Eva leaned against Tina's leg. "Are you taking Tina to a ball?"

"Um ... not really." Milo smiled, looking from Tina to Eva. "Though we are going to listen to music."

Eva nodded as if thinking that over. "You should dance with her. Princesses love to dance."

Tina closed her eyes as her face heated.

"Is that so?" Milo's jovial tone had Tina peeking one eye opened. He winked at her. "I'll have to remember that."

"So, you're a cop?" Zeke tightened his arm around Samantha's shoulder.

Did he have to talk in that intimidating tone?

"Yeah. I'm a detective with the investigations department."

Zeke nodded like he didn't already know Milo's entire history. They'd probably done a background check, complete with character references. Tina edged closer and pulled on his sleeve. She had to get him out of here.

"We should go." Tina swallowed, but it didn't help her parched throat.

"So, what kind of prince are you?" Eva's question caused Tina to groan.

"Uh ... " Milo's gaze darted around the room in question. "I'm not sure."

"Well, you're very handsome, like the prince from Sleeping Beauty, but he did nothing but sing and kiss." Eva's eyebrows furrowed. "You haven't just been singing and kissing with Tina, have you?"

Tina sputtered, and Milo's smile widened. She was glad he was enjoying this bit of torture.

"I can't sing, and there's been no kissing ... yet." Milo's eyes twinkled as his gaze flicked to her lips and back up.

Tina's knees about gave out from beneath her. Had

he been thinking about kissing her? She had ... all week long. Phew. It was getting hot. Tina nonchalantly fanned her shirt.

"Hmm ... Tina had to save you from freezing." Eva tapped her lips, and Tina rolled her eyes. "And you are a police officer, so you like to help people." One of Eva's eyebrows lifted as she thought. "You must be like Kristoff from *Frozen*, but you look more like Eric from the *Little Mermaid*. Are you a good swimmer?"

"Hookay. We're leaving now." Tina opened the door and grabbed Milo's arm.

"Nice to meet you all." Milo's voice held amusement as he followed her through the door.

Rafe prowled closer, and Tina tensed. "You hurt her, and we've got problems. Understand?"

Tina groaned, but Milo nodded. "Roger that."

"Don't forget," Eva hollered at them as Tina pulled Milo down the porch steps. "Princesses like to dance and kiss."

"Pipsqueak, we're supposed to be intimidating the man, not encouraging him." Rafe's tone was full of exasperation.

"Oh, oops. And don't be a meanie or I'll send my uncles after you." Eva's yell caused Tina to trip.

Milo wrapped his arm around her waist. Man, he smelled good. Tina peeked up at him and found him smiling down at her.

He turned back to the house and waved. "I promise, I won't be a meanie."

The front door closed, and Tina sighed in relief. How

embarrassing. Where should she even start with the apologies?

"That was fun." Milo opened the passenger door to a tall black truck, but held her waist when she tried to climb in. "So ... " His eyes darted to her lips. "Do you like ... dancing, Princess Tina?"

She swallowed hard, knowing he had to be thinking about Eva's other declaration. She sucked in a deep breath, suddenly feeling like all the air had evaporated from the atmosphere. Would he kiss her now or would she have to wait in tortured anticipation the entire night? She nodded, not able to find her voice.

His smile built slowly, sparking heat in her gut. He squeezed her waist once, the motion spreading electric tingles across her skin, then let her go. If she hadn't been holding onto the truck, she would've sunk to the ground since her knees refused to strengthen.

"Good to know." He backed up, and she stumbled into the passenger seat.

When he closed the door and walked around the front of the truck, Tina pulled in as much air as her lungs could handle. He looked at her through the windshield, a playful smile on his lips. Butterflies burst into her stomach like they'd all been just waiting for the perfect time to break from their cocoons. He could hold his own against her friends, but would she be able to hold her own against him? She shook her head and looked down at her trembling hands. Doubtful.

TWELVE

Milo watched Tina as she leaned toward the window of the gondola. She tucked her blonde hair behind her ear, revealing the graceful line of her neck and her full lips. City and Christmas lights sparkled below and reflected off the Colorado River as Glenwood got smaller and smaller the farther up the mountain they traveled, but the view had nothing on her.

He'd been a nervous wreck all week long, wondering if it was a smart idea to deviate from his plan. He'd known the second the door to the house had opened that he'd have to prove he was up to par to her friends. One look at Tina's gaze squirreling around the room told him she was just as anxious about him meeting her friends as he was. He puffed up his chest. He'd held his own and gotten permission of sorts to kiss the fair maiden.

He leaned closer, wishing there weren't other people in the gondola with them. "You've never been up here before?"

He knew the answer. He just wanted to hear her soft,

even voice. He placed his arm across the back of her seat as she turned to him.

"Nope. Just another local site your mom would be horrified that I missed as a child." She smiled at the little girl sitting across from them.

Milo cringed. "Yeah, sorry about that. She can get overzealous."

"It's okay." She bumped his side with her shoulder. "I agree with her. It's just not that fun going to these great places by yourself."

Her smile was small as she peeked up at him through her long lashes. Her eyes, warm like cinnamon, held hope and caution all mixed up. He wanted to take her all the places she'd missed out on as a kid. Wanted to erase the caution so only hope remained.

"We'll have to come back this summer so I can take you on all the rides. Most of them are closed during the winter." He pushed her hair over her shoulder.

Her eyes widened, and her chest rose in one billowing motion. "Okay."

"We also need to go back to the Hotel Colorado in the next couple of weeks. You didn't get to see the lights up close." There, he'd asked her on a follow-up date, and the first hadn't even really started yet.

"I'd like that." Her lips turned up in a small smile, before she glanced across the aisle at the family sharing the gondola car and gazed back out the window.

Milo grabbed onto her seat back so he wouldn't float to the ceiling. Why'd he wait so long to date? In truth, he hadn't met anyone like Tina before.

The gondola slowed as it came to the top of the

mountain. He wiped his palm on his pants and grabbed her hand as they proceeded off the still rotating box. She flinched, and his heart lodged in his throat. Had he overstepped?

Her fingers threaded through his, shooting warmth up his arm and jolting his heart into hyper-drive. The bite of the winter breeze blowing up the mountainside didn't even faze him.

Music from the band performing in the restaurant thudded low under the excited voices of the people milling about. The entire theme park was decked out in so many lights that even Milo was stunned. He chuckled. Guess his mom had forgotten this local gem while they were growing up. They'd always made their once a year trip to enjoy the rides during the summer, but they'd never ventured up to the park during the holidays.

"What do you want to do first? We can tour the fairy caverns, go on the alpine coaster, have dinner." He rubbed his thumb across the back of her hand. "There's also the haunted mine drop and laser tag."

"Definitely not the drop." She shivered.

What? The mighty Tina didn't want to fall?

"No? It's so thrilling though." Milo shook her hand.

"You can let the floor drop out from under you, but I think I'll stay on solid ground." She pointed to a festive Christmas display complete with fairies and reindeer. "Let's go see these fairy caves."

An hour later, after seeing the stalagmites, stalactites, and cave bacon all lighted up for the holidays, Milo pulled Tina towards the restaurant. "Dinner next, then we can race down the mountain on the coaster."

"Sounds good to me. I'm starving." Tina smiled up at him.

She'd been doing that a lot. It was distracting and tempting. More than once he'd held himself back from pulling her aside to a dark corner of the cavern and seeing if her smile tasted like the candy canes she seemed to always have.

They were enjoying the unique renditions of Christmas music the band played and were halfway through their dinner when Tina tensed across the table from him. Her normally rosy skin paled in the festive lights as she looked over his shoulder. Milo put his drink down and turned to see what had caused such a reaction.

He spotted Jase with her foster brother, Blake, and Milo's tense shoulders relaxed. He glanced back at Tina. She had scooted her chair back and was placing her napkin on the table like she was preparing to run.

Why did she react to Blake like that? Milo's eyes narrowed as he turned back to the duo. And what was Jase doing back in Glenwood? He was supposed to be in Grand Junction studying for his finals.

"Hey, you two. Imagine running into you here." Jase's false surprise had Milo clenching his hand in a fist.

The dolt knew Milo was bringing Tina here. Just what was he playing at? Blake stopped with his feet wide and his arms across his chest in a closed off stance. The hood of his black coat was bunched around his neck even though the restaurant was sweltering. He had a tightness in his eyes as he stared at Tina.

"Blake." Tina's fingers shook as she tucked her hair behind her ear.

"Hey, Tina." Blake looked towards the band, his lips pinched tight.

Just what was going on? Milo's gaze darted between the two, then landed on Jase with a raised eyebrow. Did Jase want to ruin his date?

"What are you doing back in town?" Milo couldn't help the irritated tone of his voice.

"Nice to see you too, bro." Jase rolled his eyes then clapped Blake on the shoulder. "When I heard Blake moved back to town, I had to come down and celebrate."

"You're back?" Tina's voice was high and tight.

"Yeah." Blake shrugged Jase's hand off. "Denver wasn't a good place for me to be." He nodded at Milo. "Good to see you again." He tipped his head to the bar. "I'm going to go get a drink."

He left without a word to Tina. She deflated in her chair. Her gaze staring after Blake was full of sorrow and regret. Jase had said Tina's past was difficult. Could Blake be the reason for that?

"Sorry, guys." Jase rubbed the back of his neck. "I honestly forgot you were going to be here."

"It's okay." Tina fingered her napkin where she'd tossed it on the table.

"I'll leave you two alone." Jase bumped Milo on the shoulder. "See you tomorrow."

Milo nodded, not taking his eyes off of Tina. It was like the vibrant, daring woman had shrunken to someone vulnerable and hurt. His nostrils flared as he clenched his teeth. Just what had Blake done to her?

"Can we go?" Tina cringed as she darted her gaze to the bar.

"Yeah."

Milo motioned the waitress over and handed her forty bucks. Her eyes widened when he said to keep the change. He grabbed Tina's hand and pulled her onto the deck.

"Want to tell me what that was all about?" He pulled her close as they walked towards the front of the gift shop.

She stared at the towering Christmas tree decorated in the center of the park. People milled around, children dashing this way and that with excited laughter. A Christmas song began playing from a speaker in the tree, and a small, sad smile tipped up on Tina's face.

"Blake hasn't quite forgiven me for turning our foster dad in to the cops." Tina's eyes followed a little girl as she skipped beside her father.

"Why'd you have to do that?" The mountain nachos curdled in Milo's stomach. Did he want to know the answer?

Her hand trembled in his as she swallowed hard. She gazed up at him. Her face was wary and so full of hurt he wrapped his arm around her waist.

"He—"

"Help!" A shout sounded from the path to the coaster. "Please, I can't find my nephew."

Tina jerked out of his grip and dashed toward the yelling. Milo glanced back toward the bar, then ran after her. What had she been about to say?

"He was just here." A man with wild eyes darted left and right, calling for the boy.

"Sir, what does he look like? What was he wearing?" Tina touched his arm, and the guy jerked to a stop.

"He's four-years-old, about yea high." He motioned at his hip. "He's wearing a red snow coat and a bright blue hat."

"When do you remember seeing him last?" Milo moved closer to Tina, hoping the kid had just wandered off.

"I don't know." The guy pushed his hand through his hair. "Maybe ten, fifteen minutes ago? We were all waiting for the rest of the family to get through the coaster."

A woman ran up from the area of the rides, followed by a group of kids. Her face was chalky white as she reached a shaky hand for the man's arm. Two adults brought up the rear of the group, their eyes darting from the kids in front of them to the crowd building around.

"Did you find him?" Her voice pitched high and borderline hysterical.

The man closed his eyes and shook his head. The woman choked out a sob as she clung to the man's arm.

"What seems to be the problem?" A woman in a park uniform hurried up to the crowd.

"We can't find my son." The harried mother turned on the woman like a ravenous animal, holding out her phone. A picture of a cute kid with blonde hair that flopped around his ears was on the screen.

The man with her wrapped his arm around her waist and held her back. Milo needed to take charge of the situation before the woman totally spiraled out of control. He angled towards the park worker, pulling his badge out of his pocket.

"Can you stop the gondola until we locate the boy?" Milo used his most authoritative voice.

He hated to give voice to his concern, but a chill had settled in his gut. Could there be another missing child? Hopefully, the boy had just wandered off.

"Yeah, sure thing." The worker pulled a walkie talkie to her mouth and shot the order through the radio.

"I need you eight to fan out with the family and start searching the park. Grab all the available workers and do a thorough search." Milo pointed to the workers that had gathered.

"We'll help, too." A young man with a group of friends raised his hand.

"Good. Search the dark corners and bathrooms. Maybe he's playing a game." Milo turned back to the uniformed woman. "I need to see your video feeds."

She nodded and turned towards the gift shop. Tina came beside him as they followed. Were all of their outings doomed? Jase jogged up to him from the deck stairs leading to the restaurant.

"What's going on?" He fell in with them as they followed the woman to a hall of offices at the rear of the gift shop.

"There's another kid missing." Tina's grim voice mirrored his own dread. "I wish I had Scout. I should call the ranch and have someone bring him out."

"Let's see what we find on the video. It hasn't been that long. Hopefully, the kid is still here." Milo placed his hand on her lower back as he let her lead the way into the manager's office.

It was spacious, but with the four of them in there, the room felt cramped. Or maybe it was just the thought of another kid missing that banded his chest tight. He gazed out the window that stretched across the entire wall, showcasing the sparkling town below.

"Where's Blake?" Tina's question pulled Milo's attention from the lights below.

"He bugged out right after you left." Jase chuckled. "I think you rattled him."

"It's mutual." Tina sighed.

"Okay, I have the surveillance system pulled up." The woman typed into the keyboard of her computer.

"Cue it back to the last twenty minutes. Let's focus on the gondola first." Milo leaned over the desk, hoping he was wrong.

She started playing, increasing it to double speed. The air felt pregnant with tension as people dashed across the computer. Red flashed on the screen, and Milo pointed.

"There. Back it up and slow it down." Milo's pulse roared in his ears as the boy looked up at a person leading him to the gondola.

"It's the boy." Tina's voice cracked.

"Can you pull up a video of the gondola?" Jase leaned closer.

"Yeah." She clicked, and another feed popped up.

The kid chatted happily with whoever he was with, jumping from seat to seat and peering out the window. The person who had taken the kid kept their head tucked low away from the camera. Their black hood was pulled up to hide their face.

"No." Tina gasped, gripping Milo's arm as the gondola opened and the two strolled out.

Milo pulled out his phone as the park manager clicked from feed to feed, following the kidnapper to a sage-colored Outback. He glanced at Tina as he caught Stone up on the latest abduction. Her cheek muscle jumped, and her eyes shot fire as she listened to him report to his superior. As far as first dates went, this one left a lot to be desired.

THIRTEEN

A week later, Milo scanned the busy Grand Avenue, eyeing the people rushing to their Christmas shopping and praying the sage Outback would drive by. The distraught mom of another missing kid sobbed as she gave her statement to an officer. How was it that this guy had stolen another kid? Lieutenant Stone stomped up, a scowl on his face.

"Another one?" he barked, though he knew the answer.

Milo nodded, his hand rubbing his neck.

Stone cursed low and kicked a clump of snow into the gutter. Nothing ever rattled him, but then again, they'd never had to deal with a spree of kidnapped children. He motioned for Milo to follow and headed down the sidewalk.

"What do we know?" Stone stopped a few stores down, glancing back at the mother.

"Not much." Milo ground his teeth. "The kidnapper drives a sage older model Outback."

Stone groaned and rubbed his hand down his face. "Half of Garfield County has that car."

"He's getting bolder, taking the kid in broad daylight." Milo motioned at the busy street. "Callahan's back at the precinct going through traffic videos. Maybe we'll get lucky."

"What about the storefronts' surveillance?" Stone pointed to buildings.

"I have officers going to businesses, but almost all of the buildings are managed by leasing companies. It'll take time tracking down the videos."

Milo's stomach growled loudly, and Stone's eyebrow rose. "When was the last time you ate?"

Milo shrugged. He'd had a Poptart on the way into the precinct. Eating didn't seem important when children were missing. His eyelids gritted like sandpaper as he blinked. Too many late nights trying to track down the kidnapper.

Three kids in three weeks. He'd spent the entire week scouring the video feeds from both crimes and had nothing they could go on. They'd likely never find the children alive.

Was it wrong that he'd been praying for a trafficking ring rather than a homicidal psychopath? At least then they might find them. The sickening fear that had plagued him since Thanksgiving soured his gut. Even then, the kids were probably long gone. That whoever was doing this would choose the holidays just showed how heartless they were.

"I've called Tina. She's bringing Scout down." Milo sighed, the weight of not finding the kids bent his shoulders. "Maybe they can give us something to work with."

"When you're done here, I want you to take the rest of the day off."

"But, sir--"

"Bishop, you've been going nonstop for a week. I need you at a hundred percent." Stone crossed his arms. "You're taking the rest of the day off and that's an order."

It didn't seem right to not go down to the precinct, but Milo also knew exhaustion was fraying his brain. Maybe he could go home and pull up the case on his laptop.

"So, you and Tina West?" Stone smiled smugly before he sobered. "I've known that girl forever. She was always so quiet, but I guess after what happened to her parents it's not a surprise. Always figured she'd become an accountant or librarian, something calm, not S&R."

Milo's mind reeled with all Stone just said. Milo had spent a night freezing in a tent with her, gone on two, well, one and a half dates and still knew next to nothing about her and her past. How was it that both his brother and his boss kept stringing Milo along with just enough info to drive a man crazy? He grabbed onto one statement, hoping to get something, anything from him.

"How do you know her?"

"Her foster dad, John, was my best friend." Stone grimaced, his feet shuffling in the dirty snow. "I ... I let her down when she needed someone. She might not be happy to see me."

"What happened?" Milo was too warm, his coat

stuffy as Stone pulled at his collar. Did Milo want to know?

"She had a foster sister who was a few months older than her. They were best friends. Closer than most sisters. Faith was her name." Stone's face filled with sadness. "John abused her, coming into her room at night after everyone else was in bed."

"Tina?" Milo could barely force the question out.

"No." Stone's quick answer whooshed a sudden release of tension through Milo. "Faith stacked up a lot of evidence, catching John on video night after night. She left it all and a note for Tina to find before she killed herself."

The lump in Milo's throat grew uncomfortable as he tried to swallow it down. Poor Tina. He remembered the case now. It was the year after Jase had graduated, and he'd been upset about it. Milo had been so focused on his job and moving up into the investigations department, that he hadn't connected the death to Jase's best friend, Blake. He figured the girl had just been a friend, someone Jase had known from high school.

For someone who prided himself in his attention to detail, Milo seemed to miss a lot back then. How had he not known Blake lived with other foster kids? How had Milo never connected the girl's suicide to Blake? What else had Milo missed in his tunnel vision?

"I think Tina blamed me." Stone cleared his throat. "Shoot. I blamed myself." He cleared his throat again, looking down to his feet before bringing his gaze to Milo. "Anyway, your mom says she seems to be doing good."

Milo's skin itched at the reference to his mom. He

still hadn't gotten used to her and Stone dating. Not that Milo didn't like Stone. Just the opposite. Stone had a dangerous job still working in the field. Milo couldn't see his mom hurt again.

"Yeah, she seems to be."

Did Milo even know? Every time he was with her, their time turned chaotic. Was this a sign from above that maybe Milo should stick with the plan to not mess with dating until Jase finished with school?

"Milo!" Tina's shout from down the block turned both Milo and Stone.

Her cheeks were flushed pink as she rushed down the sidewalk. She held his gaze, her eyes filled with determination. She was beautiful, reminding him of an avenging angel. Maybe them being thrown together in these situations was a sign that Milo should stick it out. God abhorred innocents being hurt and stolen, but maybe He kept pulling Tina and Milo together because He knew how thick-headed Milo was.

His heart thudded in his chest like a hammer striking an anvil as she approached. "Hey. Thanks for coming."

"Glad to help." She turned to Stone, her expression hesitant. "Hey, Mr. Stone."

"It's Jeff, and it's nice to see you, Tina." His smile was strained as he placed a hand on her shoulder, quickly taking it off to point at the dog. "This must be the impressive Scout."

"Yep. He's the muscle and the brains of our operation. I just hold the leash." She patted him lovingly on the side before penetrating Milo with a questioning stare. "Another kid's been taken?"

Milo nodded, frustration hardening in his gut. "Yeah. We're hoping you and Scout can give us a direction to look. Maybe by following Scout's trail, we can narrow down the video feeds we need to search."

"What do we have for Scout to use?" Tina's relaxed posture eased some of Milo's tension.

He handed her the plastic bag with a cloth baby doll in it. The tension returned as she blinked the brightness from her eyes. Did this hit too close to home for her? He wanted to dig, to discover everything about her, but that would have to wait.

She opened the bag and held it up to Scout's nose. "Go find her."

Scout's tail wagged as he sniffed the air, the end of his nose moving this way and that. He froze, and Milo held his breath. Then Scout darted down the sidewalk, his tail held high in the air. Five minutes later, in a parking spot along the side of the road, Scout lay down with a whine.

Milo scanned the historic houses lining Colorado Avenue. Hope pushed through the cold lodged in his chest. With businesses set up in a lot of the old homes up and down this street and it being the middle of the day, there was a chance the kidnapper had been caught on video.

He squeezed Tina's hand as she waited for Scout to bring back the ball. "This is good. We have a lot to go on now."

"I hope so." Tina pinched her lips together. "I just wish we could do more."

"Yeah, me too." Milo shook her hand. "Listen, Stone

is forcing me to take the rest of the day off, and I'm starving. Want to grab something to eat when I'm done here?"

He held his breath as she let go of his hand to reward Scout with a hug. An eternity passed before her soft "okay" floated up to him. The slight lift of her lips sent warmth straight to his gut. Stone was right. Taking the night off might be just what Milo needed.

FOURTEEN

Tina peeked over at Milo as they walked to her car to put Scout in his kennel. Another date? Would this one end as depressingly as the last one?

She scoffed to herself. This one started out depressing. Couldn't get any worse, could it?

She pulled up short as Blake hurried out of the á la carte boutique. What in the world was her brother doing in a froo-frooey store? His eyes went wide as he stumbled to a stop, shoving the plastic shopping bag in the pocket of his oversized black coat.

"Tina. Milo. Out on another date?" He shuffled from side to side like he had in high school when he'd done something wrong.

Tina narrowed her eyes. Just what was he up to? Scout inched up to him and sniffed his shoes.

Blake froze, his hands held out to his side. "Your dog won't bite me, right?"

"Depends." Tina loved getting back at him for all the times he'd tormented her.

Blake's eyes stretched to the max, and his Adam's apple bobbed. Milo turned his face away, rubbing his hand across a smile he hadn't been quick enough to hide. Tina snickered.

Despite all that had happened, she had missed Blake. She hadn't just lost Faith three years ago, she'd lost Blake, her foster mom, Susan, and the only sense of home she'd ever had. Sure, she went to visit Susan a few times a year, but it wasn't the same.

"Relax, Blake. Scout won't hurt you." Tina smiled, and Blake let his arms drop to his sides. "Unless you run. Then he'll hunt you down, possibly take off an arm."

Milo chuckled, shaking his head. "Man, you should've seen your face."

"Whatever." Blake rolled his eyes, taking a small step back as Scout sniffed up his leg. "What are you guys up to?"

"Just got off a crime scene. Another abducted kid." Milo glanced over his shoulder at the cops still processing the scene.

Blake grimaced. "Really? That's too bad."

He didn't sound all that sincere, but then again, he'd never had much sympathy for others. Scout sniffed Blake's hand, and Blake flinched. Scout's ears lay flat against his head, a low growl coming from him.

Blake froze. "I thought you said he wouldn't bite?"

Tina called Scout off. The dog looked from Blake to Tina like he questioned her command to stand down. A knot twisted in her gut. Just what was Blake doing back in town? After their foster dad had been thrown in jail, Blake had said he'd never return.

"Well, listen. I gotta run." Blake inched backwards. "I've ... I've got an interview I need to get to."

"All right." Tina spoke slowly, carefully weighing what to say. "It was good to see you again."

"Yeah, sure." Blake waved. "See ya."

He practically jogged to the corner and turned left on Eighth. Scout huffed and peered up at Tina like she'd just made a colossal mistake. What if she had? Blake had always teetered on the side of legal, playing pranks and partying in high school. Had he tipped all the way down that trail?

"That was weird." Milo shoved his hands in his pockets. "Think he's in trouble?"

"I don't know." Tina sighed and continued to the car. "I haven't seen him in three years, and we didn't leave on pleasant terms."

"What happened?"

"He blamed me for our foster dad going to jail."

"How in the world could he blame you for that?" Milo's voice hardened. "Your foster dad deserved it."

The traffic blared in her ears, and an icy wind slapped her face. "So you know?"

"Not really. Not all of it." Milo shrugged. "Stone said he'd let you down. When I asked why, he told me about Faith and what had happened." He placed his hand on her arm as they waited for the light at the crosswalk. "I'm sorry you had to go through that."

"No, he didn't let me down. John duped us all."

Tina's eyes blurred with tears, and she turned her head away. She hadn't talked about it to anyone, not since she'd handed over the videos to the police. She had thought it a blessing that her eighteenth birthday had been in January, so she could be on her own, not being forced to see the psychiatrist the state wanted her to talk to.

A loud beeping jerked her back, and she plodded into the street. She glanced at Milo, his hands swinging loosely at his side and his gaze alert as he scanned the area. She sensed she could trust him. Maybe it was time she spoke with someone. At least, it'd tell her if Milo would stick around or not.

"I—" She cleared her throat, tucking her hair behind her ear. "I loved it at the Harris's. My childhood wasn't filled with sunshine and roses. My father was an abusive drunk, so I spent a lot of time at friends' houses."

She laughed, but there was no joy behind it. "I'd rotate homes so my friends' parents didn't catch on." She stopped in front of the coffee shop and peered up at Milo, who met her gaze. "Kind of sad that a seven-year-old would know to do that, huh?"

His eyebrows furrowed over blue eyes that held sorrow. He nodded and pushed her hair over her shoulder. "Yeah."

The touch brought a comfort Tina couldn't explain, a warmth that pushed the frigidness from her veins. He dropped his hand like he realized what he had done. His fingers opened and closed by his side.

She took a deep breath, wanting the solace his presence brought. She slid her hand down his arm and threaded her fingers through his. He held tight, like maybe he needed the connection as much as she did. She continued down the sidewalk towards her car.

"When I was nine, my dad got in one of his rages. He killed my mom, then killed himself." She couldn't look at Milo as she spoke. "Probably would've killed me too if I'd been home."

"I'm sorry, Tina."

She hadn't thought about her parents. It was callous of her, but she'd just been an inconvenience to them. Her mom had blamed Tina for her father's drunkenness. Her father had just seen her as something else to punch.

"They weren't really parents, more like selfish children." Tina huffed. "I would've been taken away from the house years before if anyone had noticed what was going on. Maybe that would've been better for everyone."

"Didn't you have other family to go to?"

"No." She kicked a chunk of snow down the sidewalk. "My dad met my mom while he backpacked through Sweden. My mom hated her parents, and my dad's parents died when I was young. I wouldn't have wanted to live with them, anyway. Let's just say the apple hadn't fallen far from the tree."

She stopped beside her car parked on Seventh. She had told this much, she might as well spill it all. She tried to smile at Scout as he sniffed the air with a cheerful look on his face.

"I bounced around the foster system until I landed at the Harris's when I was thirteen." She stared at their joined hands. "It was the first place that had felt like home. Blake was already there. He'd been with the Harris's for three years. Faith arrived a couple of weeks after I did. In no time, it felt like we were an actual family."

She closed her eyes, her nose stinging. "I'd never had that before."

Her chest was tight with the memory. Would her happiness always be tainted with such pain? Milo's feather-soft touch brushed against her cheek. Her eyes snapped open as she touched her fingertips to her cold, wet skin. When had the tears escaped? Scout whined at her side, leaning into her.

"You don't have to talk about it anymore if you don't want to." Worry and pain laced Milo's voice.

His concern gave her the courage to push forward. "Susan had always wanted kids, but they couldn't for some reason. Since they couldn't afford to adopt, she signed them up for fostering." She swallowed. "John, though firm in how he wanted things done around the house, had always seemed indifferent. Not mean or anything, just unconcerned about us, or at least he always seemed indifferent to me. Guess I was wrong about that."

Tina smiled a genuine smile. "Susan, on the other hand, was amazing, a true June Cleaver type of mom. She showered us with love and cookies, such good home-cooked meals that I never asked to eat out. I talked to her about everything." Her face heated as she glanced up at him. "Even my crush on you."

"Me?" Milo pointed at his chest.

"Yeah." Tina chuckled. "It was silly, especially with me being a freshman and you being a senior. But Susan comforted me when my tender heart was crushed."

"How did I crush your heart?" His words stuttered out, and he moved closer. "I think I'd remember going to school with you, freshman or not."

She shrugged. "I was geeky in school, wore these enormous glasses that hid my face." A laugh forced out. "You talked to me once in the library. I was so stunned, I gaped like an idiot. I was mortified. When I got home, I cried into my pillows. I stopped stalking you during study hour after that, preferring to hide with good ol' Brittanica."

"That was you?" He closed the space between them, his hand sliding up her shoulder and behind her neck.

His closeness fled all thought from her brain, just like it had that day in the library. She nodded, her throat too thick to speak. A slow, delicious smile built on his lips.

"Do you know how long it took me to get up the nerve to talk to you that day?" His words forced a gasp from her.

"What?"

"I'd watched you for weeks. When you'd blushed so prettily, I thought maybe I had a chance." He brushed his thumb along her jaw as his fingers cupped the back of her neck. "I could never find you after that day. I was so disappointed."

"I ... I—" Her eyes had frozen open, so shocked she couldn't blink.

"What are the chances we'd meet again?" He leaned closer, his warm breath smelled like Juicy Fruit. "I wish you hadn't hidden from me."

He stood so close his heat radiated to her. Would he kiss her? Why wait to find out? Tina stood on her tiptoes and pressed her lips to his. Her pulse pounded in her neck, and she was positive he could feel it against his thumb as it stroked down her skin.

He smiled against her mouth as he speared his fingers through her hair. He wasn't running away, wasn't scared of her past. Goosebumps slid along her neck as his fingers glided on her scalp. Hope unlike any she'd ever felt before burned hot in her stomach, spreading warmth through her body. She fisted her fingers into his leather coat and dove in for another kiss.

FIFTEEN

Milo studied the latest video for the hundredth time, praying he'd catch something he'd missed. He rubbed his dry eyes before pushing back from his desk with a huff. He'd been staring at the screen too long. He needed to move, needed fresh air to jolt his system back awake. Since he wasn't leaving the office until he found a new lead, coffee would have to do.

Stalking to the coffee machine, he filled his mug. His nose wrinkled as the smell of old brew steamed off his mug. He should make more. He lifted the pot up with a scowl. Still half full. He slammed it back on the coffeemaker. He'd just have to drink it faster.

He took his mug and stood before the crazy wall where they had the abductions mapped out. They didn't have much to go on. The kidnapper drove an Outback and wore a large black coat with the hood pulled up. Large families seemed the targets since the kids had all been lured from groups. All the videos showed the kids going willingly with the abductor, so he must appear friendly. The guy wasn't huge, maybe five-seven.

The only new info they had to go on was he lived in Glenwood, or at least he was staying in town. They'd been able to track the car to where it turned off of Grand. There were so many neighborhoods spread out in that area, it'd take weeks to canvas them all. At least, they knew the kids were staying in Glenwood, however temporarily.

Milo cringed as he took a drink of the bitter coffee. Maybe he would make a new pot. If he let the current one sit any longer, it'd turn to ash.

He turned to the coffeemaker only to stop short as Jase sauntered into the office. Milo's eyes narrowed, and he slammed the mug onto his desk. Jase was supposed to be at school taking his finals.

"Jase, what are you doing here?" Milo crossed his arms over his chest, hating that he sounded like a disgruntled father.

He was tired of being the responsible one. Tired of his brother throwing Milo's sacrifice in his face every chance Jase got. Milo rubbed his hand over the back of his neck. That wasn't fair. He was glad Jase got experiences he never had, like college and having fun.

"Nice to see you, too." Jase clapped Milo on the shoulder. "You look rough, man. You sleeping here or what?"

"Nah." Well, kind of. He'd come in at three when he couldn't fall back to sleep. "Just a rough case is all."

Jase's eyebrows drew together as he peered at the

crazy wall. "Still haven't tracked down the jerk taking the kids?"

"No. And he's getting bolder." Milo leaned against his desk with a sigh. "Took the last kid in broad daylight."

"And you can't track where he goes?"

"As soon as he turns off the main road, we lose him." Milo crossed his arms again.

"Too bad Scout can't track cars." Jase leaned against Callahan's desk, his head tilting to the side. "You went on another date last night?"

"How'd you know?"

"I have my ways." He cocked an eyebrow. "So, how's it going? You kiss her yet?"

The feel of her soft hair tangled around his fingers came rushing back. He'd been able to keep his mind off of the touch of her lips and the way she'd held on to his coat for most of the morning. That one small question from Jase had Milo overheating and his fingers itching to slide back into her hair.

"Hoo-hoo! That's a yes." Jase's smug smile turned into a full-on grin as he rubbed his hands together.

"I didn't say anything." Milo reached for his mug and grimaced as he swallowed the lukewarm drink.

"You didn't have to, bro. It's written all over your face."

Jase rearranged the items on Callahan's desk and plopped himself down on it. Maybe she'd come back from lunch and ream him out for messing with her stuff. That would be more enjoyable than his brother's prodding.

"When I talked to Blake, he said he'd run into you

two again, I knew it had to be getting serious." Jase picked up a Scooby-Doo action figure and examined it with a smirk.

"We've been on two dates. I wouldn't call that getting serious."

Though after their conversation over dinner, how they'd talked about the darkness of their pasts and the hopes of the future, he could admit to not wanting whatever it was between them to fizzle out. He still couldn't believe he'd told her about his father's murder and the weight of responsibility he felt. However, after she'd shared about herself, he wanted to trust her with his history.

"You were out on a weekday, Milo." Jase put Scooby down and picked up Velma. "You never do fun on a weekday. Shoot, you don't do fun on the weekend, either."

Milo let that comment slide. "So, Blake told you?"

"Yeah." Jase tossed Velma up and caught her. "Something's off about him. It has me worried."

"Like what?"

"I don't know, man. He hasn't talked to me about it." He moved Velma's arms like she was talking. "I think maybe he got himself into trouble in Denver." Jase shrugged. "He's not acting like himself."

"Jase," Stone hollered from his office door. "Come on in."

Milo's blood froze in his veins as his gaze darted from Stone to Jase. "Just what are you doing here, Jase? Why aren't you back at school?"

Jase looked towards Stone's office, not meeting Milo's

glare causing his heart to thump in his chest. "I had my last final yesterday." Jase sighed and met Milo's gaze head on. "I'm not going back. After Christmas, I head to the academy. I'm joining the force."

"No, Jase. You don't want to be a cop." How had Milo not known about this? "You need to stay in school and get your degree."

"I've been thinking about this for a while now, Milo." Jase clenched the doll still in his hand. "I shifted my major to criminal justice a year and a half ago, double upped on classes. Don't worry. I got my degree. Stone says that depending on how training goes, I might have my pick of departments."

"But — " Milo's world was caving in around him.

Jase couldn't be a cop. Couldn't put himself in danger like that every day. What would Mom think? It was bad enough that she could lose Milo at any time, but adding Jase to that risk was more than she should have to bear.

"I thought you wanted to go into law?" That was a safe job.

"What are you doing?" Callahan's steely voice shot through the office.

Jase froze, his eyes widening as Callahan stomped across the office and ripped the Velma doll from his hand. With her fist on her hips and her cowgirl boots planted wide, Jase didn't have a chance of talking his way out of the lashing sure to come.

"I'm Jase, Milo's brother." Jase's hands gripped the side of the desk.

"That's nice. Now, get off my desk." Callahan tossed Velma with the rest of the gang.

A slow smile built on Jase's face. "Not until you tell me your name."

Man, his brother had guts. Few went up against Callahan. With her cowgirl tough attitude and inability to back down, most of the other officers steered clear of her.

She turned her glare on Milo. "Is he for real?"

"Yeah." Milo shrugged. "He's an idiot."

She smirked and turned back to Jase, crossing her arms over her chest. "The name's Dusty. Now, get off my desk before I pull your arm out of socket and slap you with it."

"Jase." Stone's sharp command pushed Jase's smile higher.

"Looks like I'll be seeing you around, Dusty." Jase pushed off the desk into Callahan's space.

When she didn't step back, his eyebrows cocked up. Oh, brother. Milo shook his head.

"Catch you later, bro." Jase stared at Callahan as he spoke, then strode towards Stone's office.

Callahan gazed after him until the door closed with a snap. She jerked and let out a huff before slapping her stuff back into place on her desk. Not good. Not good at all. Milo didn't need any additional drama in his life, especially between his partner and brother.

Jase, a cop? Milo groaned as he sulked to the coffeepot. How had all his plans gotten so out of whack?

SIXTEEN

"Come on, Tina, you can do this." Tina gripped the steering wheel as she stared at her foster mom, Susan's, house.

She'd put off coming to visit too long, letting guilt coat her tongue and churn her stomach. Why did she always wait until she was miserable before she came by? Why couldn't she just move past what had happened within the walls of the cute ranch-style house?

She didn't have to let the horror of Faith's abuse and death affect her anymore. Didn't have to let it slick her palms with sweat at the thought of stepping through the door. The monster responsible for the atrocities was rotting in prison for the rest of his life, so it wasn't like Tina had to be scared that she'd be attacked.

Poor Susan's life had been ruined. She rarely left home for fear of what people would say. Tina had had to dig deep to realize that Susan wasn't to blame for what had happened. She was so full of love and innocence that she had never imagined her husband John could do such an appalling thing.

The curtain moved in the living room window. Nuts. Looked like Tina's waffling was up. She grabbed the Christmas present from the passenger seat and pushed the door open.

Each step felt heavier than the last as she trudged up the walkway. "Please, Lord, please help me get through this."

God would helped Tina find forgiveness and reconciliation with Susan. He could take away the fear that strangled Tina every time she came over. She should try harder to convince Susan to go out to eat or shop or anything besides meeting here. The bright teal door that had always seemed so cheerful swung open as Tina reached up to knock.

"Tina, what a surprise." Susan fingered her necklace, nerves radiating off her and smacking Tina in the gut. "I didn't know you were coming today."

"Yeah, sorry. I meant to come earlier this month, but I've been busy." *Liar, liar. Pants on fire.*

Tina shifted from one foot to the other as she stared at Susan. Had Tina offended Susan so much that she wouldn't let her in?

Tina swallowed, her eyes widening as she remembered the last time they'd seen each other. How had she forgotten about the argument they'd gotten into? Tina had told Susan that if she wanted to move on, she needed to sell the house and start fresh. It was the first time she had raised her voice in anger at Tina. She'd called to apologize, but maybe Susan was still upset.

After everything that had happened to her, Susan had been the only one who had filled that mother role. Tina bit her lip. She needed to do a better job at showing Susan what that meant to her.

"I got you a present." Tina forced a smile.

"Well ... " Susan glanced back into the house. "Well, I guess you can come in real quick."

She jerked back and motioned in. Tina entered the house, her movements stiff with hurt at Susan's words. Why did Tina keep messing up relationships that mattered to her?

The house smelled like fresh baked snickerdoodles. They were Susan's favorite, and the cinnamon goodness had often filled the house when Tina was a teen. Susan's coat and purse were draped over the couch haphazardly like she hadn't had enough time to put them away. Had Tina just popped in at the wrong time, flustering Susan? It didn't take much to do that these last few years.

Ribbons, garland, and Christmas merriment dotted every surface and graced every window and doorway. Tina hadn't seen the house decorated since that horrible year Faith died. Hopefully, it meant Susan was healing and moving on with her life.

A noise sounded down the hall toward the bedrooms, pulling Tina's attention from the Snoopy figurines gracing their spot on the counter. Did Susan have company? Is that why she had hesitated to let Tina in?

"Darn cat." Susan laughed weakly. "I just got him, but he keeps going after the decorations." She reached for her necklace before jerking her hand down. "Listen, Tina honey, I hate to be rude, but Blake is going to be here any minute and, well, I know how you two don't get along anymore."

"Oh, okay." Tina set her gift on the counter. "I guess I should've called before I came over."

"No worries." Susan grabbed two cookies and wrapped them in a napkin. "Maybe we can meet for coffee soon."

She placed the cookies in Tina's hand and ushered her towards the door. Another crash sounded, and a yowl came from the hall. A shiver started at the base of her neck and skittered down her spine. She hated this house.

"I should've waited to get a cat until after Christmas." Susan pushed harder on Tina. "The silly thing hates being locked in the back room."

"That's obvious."

"Oh." Susan reached for a small package on the entry table. "This is for you. Merry Christmas, honey."

Tina took the present and tried not to flinch when Susan gave her an awkward hug. Tina hadn't even made it a step away before the door slammed shut behind her. Her eyes stung, and she pressed her lips tight together as she made her way back to the car. She tucked the present into her coat pocket and pulled out her keys.

When she opened the door, Scout whined and scratched at his kennel. Could he tell that the visit had upset her?

Blake pulled in just as Tina got ready to climb into her seat. Nuts. She hadn't left fast enough.

Blake gave her a hesitant wave as he parked next to her in the driveway. He cut the engine, the door to his beat-up Chevy truck squeaking as he opened it. His gaze darted to the house before he nodded at her.

"Tina."

"Blake."

"Susan asked if I'd help her set up a Christmas tree she just bought." Blake scratched his jaw. "Said she decided to go real this year."

"It's good she's decorating again."

"Yeah."

Tina fiddled with the napkin, wondering what she should say. She didn't want Blake upset with her anymore. Though they were completely opposite, they had always had fun ribbing each other and hanging out when he wasn't with his friends.

She cleared her throat. "I'm glad you're back."

His eyes widened as they shot to her. "You are?"

"Yeah." She shrugged. "Maybe we can hang out with Milo and Jase sometime. I'd like to catch up."

"Sure." He swallowed, before leaning on the roof of her car. "I'm surprised you like Milo. He's pretty controlling, kind of like dad was."

Scout growled low from his kennel, giving her an excuse to not reply to his comment that left her brain stumbling. Was Milo like their foster dad? She didn't think so, but then again, she hadn't seen John Harris for the monster he was either.

Tina peeked through the window at the kennel. The dog stared at Blake through the wire, his teeth bared. What was going on with Scout? He let out a sharp bark, and Tina flinched.

Blake stepped back. "That dog doesn't like me."

"Sorry about that." Tina cringed and shushed Scout. "I better go."

"Okay. See you around." Blake waved again as he passed the hood of the car.

Tina slid into the seat, her hands trembling from Blake's implications. "Scout, what has gotten into you?"

Scout whined from the back and scratched at the kennel again. Something was up with her dog. Was it just her and Blake's strained relationship Scout was picking up on? Was Blake right, and Scout didn't like him? Maybe the poor dog was just worried about her. She'd been rattled the last few weeks.

Her phone dinged with a text. She pulled it from her purse, her fingers losing feeling as she read the message from Milo. He needed her to meet him at the Christmas tree farm. Another child had been taken.

Tina squeezed her eyes shut, willing the dread to settle. Would she and Scout be able to find clues this time, or would they come up empty again? Maybe Scout needed to go to someone who was better trained and less an emotional wreck, someone who actually knew what they were doing. The thought of finding him another home made it hard to breathe. She jammed the key into the ignition and backed out, Scout whining as they left.

SEVENTEEN

"I don't understand. Why would someone take a child right before Christmas?" The mother of the latest abducted child motioned wildly like she expected some divine answer.

There was no way Milo could reply without sounding short-tempered. His anger and helplessness warred within him for action. They'd done everything they could to find this guy. Had officers questioning all those on their list of owners of the car model, even randomly stopping Outbacks and patrolling the neighborhoods where the car disappeared. Nothing.

"People who do these kinds of things don't care about holidays or decentness." Callahan answered the mom, a bite to her tone.

Was his partner as frustrated as he was? Her fingers held her pen tight, her knuckles turning white as she took down the information. Yep, she felt it, too.

"You've had four weeks to catch this person. Four weeks!" The dad shouted, his face turning red. "And now my daughter is missing because you couldn't do your job!"

Milo barely bit back the retort that the dad should've been keeping a better eye on his kid. "We've been working non-stop on this, sir. I promise you, we will do everything we can to get your daughter back to you."

What a hollow promise that was. Milo swallowed down acidic desperation as it bubbled up his throat. Tires crunched in the parking lot. Tina pulled into an unoccupied spot, and the tightness in his shoulders released.

"I'm going to bring Tina up to speed." Milo nodded toward her vehicle, heading off as quickly as he could—running away from the anger of the parents.

Great. Not only was he a liar, but he was also a chicken. Maybe he wasn't cut out for the investigations department. Milo stomped through the Christmas tree farm, his mind stewing.

Tina clicked the leash on Scout and nodded to Milo. "Hey."

"Another girl's been taken." Milo's frustration boiled over, and he kicked the tire. "Everywhere we turn, we come up empty. I don't even know why I called you out here. It's not like you can help."

Tina flinched. Why was he taking it out on her? His chin dropped to his chest. She didn't deserve him spewing all over her.

"I'm sorry, Tina."

He met her hooded gaze. She shrugged, scanning the field of Christmas trees. The festive music that played over a speaker from the store grated in his ears. He wasn't a huge fan of Christmas music to begin with, but the annoying rendition of *Jingle Bells* pushed his headache to migraine level.

"Do you want us to look or not?" Tina patted Scout's side, not looking at Milo.

He'd messed up. "Yeah. Hopefully, the kid just wandered off too far."

He handed her the plastic bag with a *unicorn* stocking cap in it. She took it without touching him and extended it to Scout. His heart beat sluggishly in his chest. If he didn't knock off his attitude, he'd screw things up with her for good.

Scout sniffed the air and immediately headed through the trees. Milo kept pace with Tina as she followed Scout. The crisp air fairly snapped with tension as the silence built between them. Milo had to fix this.

He moved closer so their arms brushed as they walked. "Look, Tina, I'm really sorry." He rubbed the back of his neck. "I'm ... this case ... we can't seem to catch a break. I'm just beyond frustrated. I shouldn't have snapped at you, not when you've gone out of your way to help us."

"I get it." Tina sighed. "I wish we could help more." She peeked up at him, hurt still banked in her eyes. "I may have been a little touchy. I haven't had the best day, either."

She focused back on Scout, giving him encouragement. Milo glanced around to make sure no one was watching. Since they had ventured further back in the lot where it was free of roaming shoppers, he shifted closer. He brushed his hand against hers.

"What happened?"

"I went to see Susan, my foster mom." She sniffed. "She practically kicked me out of the house."

"She was mad?"

"No ... just didn't want me there." Her eyes blinked like she kept tears at bay.

"I'm sorry." He hooked his fingers to hers.

"Blake showed up to help her put up her tree." She shrugged. "Maybe she just didn't want the tension between Blake and me."

"That's probably it." Milo gave a tiny shake of her hand, glad she hadn't pulled away yet.

"He said ... " Tina darted her eyes to him. Her cheeks pinked. "That is, I told him we should get together, me, you, him, and Jase."

"Okay."

"I don't want things to be strained between us anymore. We were friends before everything happened." Tina stopped as Scout sniffed a tree. "Maybe with you and your brother there, it won't be so awkward."

"Since Jase is moving back and joining the police force, getting together might not be too hard now." Milo couldn't keep the aggravation from his voice.

"You're not happy about that?"

"I ... I just wish he had decided to become a lawyer like he'd wanted when he first went to college." The headache that had eased as they had talked reared back. "Police work isn't the safest job out there."

"Yet, you do it."

"Yeah. I just hope he doesn't come in all hot-headed and get in too deep."

They emerged out into a different parking lot. Scout

went down to his belly and whined, pawing at the snow before him. Milo growled. When would they catch a break? Tina dropped Milo's hand and rewarded Scout with enthusiasm.

Milo put his fists on his hips and glanced around. Just where were they? A young man wearing an elf hat appeared from the trees twenty feet away, his keys twirling around his finger.

"Hey." Milo flashed his badge. "What is this lot used for?"

The kid's eyebrows flew to his forehead before he stuttered out a response. "It's employee parking, sir."

"Thanks." Milo dismissed him with a wave and stalked to where Tina threw a ball for Scout. "Dead end. Again."

Tina's shoulders slumped. "How did the guy even know about this lot?"

"Who knows. This guy is smart." Milo motioned to the few cars parked there, surrounded by Christmas trees on one side and a field on the other. "There's no way to know if it's the same person. No cameras back here."

"Can you look at the traffic cams? Maybe follow him home?" Tina gazed at him in hope.

"We can try to pick the car up back in town, but if it's like before, we'll lose him when he turns off Grand. There aren't any cameras covering the residential streets." He clenched his jaw, and pain exploded in his head. Would they ever locate these kids?

"I can see if Rafe can find anything out." Tina tucked her hair behind her ear before tossing the toy into the field. "The guys have access to satellites and whatnot from their time in special ops. They might find some info the cameras are missing."

"Okay. Thanks." Milo's chest tightened with the inability to find these children. "I'll take whatever help I can get. If they're still out there, I want these kids home before Christmas."

Tina pulled out her phone and paced to the edge of the field that Scout had disappeared into. Milo turned in a circle, the beauty of the snow-covered trees and towering mountains doing nothing to lift his spirits. He glared down the small driveway leading to the county road as if he stared long enough, the missing children would materialize out of thin air.

What if they never found the kids?

What if the kidnapper had already shipped them off to where they were being sold or whatever it was they were being trafficked for?

What if...

Milo swallowed the bile that rose up his throat. What if they were already dead, and all they'd find were bodies? *Lord, please.* The prayer dried up with an inability to form the words. It didn't matter. God knew the prayers Milo's heart couldn't express.

Milo motioned to Tina to head back through the farm. He couldn't rely on prayers alone. He had work to do, and he couldn't do that standing around here.

EIGHTEEN

Tina trudged up the steps to the apartment above the garage she shared with Samantha and Eva. She had been no help to the case, not really. She had brought Rafe up to speed, and he'd promised to see what he could find. The problem was finding sometimes took time.

Time for those children to disappear forever.

She punched the door's key code in with harder force than necessary and entered the apartment. She needed a steaming bath, a cup of tea, and to snuggle in bed with a thrilling mystery movie. Scratch that. Maybe a home improvement show would be better right now. The one with those cute twins. Something where she wouldn't have to think or watch some lovey-dovey couple make moon eyes at each other.

Blake's comment about Milo being like their foster dad replayed in her head. Milo had seemed like a different person when she pulled up. Was it the case or had she gotten a peek into his true nature?

"Tina!" Eva dashed through the living room and jumped into Tina's arms.

Tina buried her nose into Eva's hair and inhaled. She smelled of cinnamon and vanilla, just like Susan's house. Tina's nose stung. She scrunched it as she pulled herself together.

"We made sneaky doodles!" Eva wiggled to get down, grabbed Tina's hand, and pulled her to the bar counter. "You have to try them."

Instrumental Christmas music played softly over the speakers. The Christmas tree blinked merrily before the large window. The scent of spices and sugar filled the room. Would Tina ever enjoy the beauty of this season again?

Samantha scooped cookies off of a baking sheet, while Zeke watched like every move she made was enthralling. Tina tried not to be jealous that they'd found happiness together. She succeeded, most of the time. Sometimes, though, seeing the three of them become more of a family every day made Tina's heart ache with what if's.

What if she had made a mistake getting her hopes up with Milo?

What if no one ever looked at her like Zeke looked at Samantha?

What if Tina never had a family of her own?

The questions were piling up, making her wonder if she'd be better off somewhere else than here. She hated when her thoughts went down that trail. Deep in her heart, the Stryker ranch was the place she wanted to be the most. She saw her potential budding here, more than anywhere she'd ever been.

Felt herself ... or what she imagined herself to be.

"They're called snickerdoodles, Eva." Samantha rolled her eyes, a smile stretched wide upon her face.

Eva shook her head. "Well, I think they should be called sneaky doodles because they look all boring until you take a bite. Then — blam — they sneak up on you with yumminess."

Zeke chuckled. The look was good on his normally serious face. "I think you like them called sneaky because you want to sneak extras." Zeke snagged a cookie from the plate and bit half of it off.

Eva's hands covered her mouth to hide her giggle. Sam gasped and playfully swatted his arm with the spatula. The merry picture left a hollowness in Tina's chest.

"I'm going to head into my room." Tina rubbed her sleeve. "It's been a tough afternoon."

"Another one?" Zeke's eyebrows pulled together.

"Yeah."

She'd leave it at that. No use telling them that her time at Susan's shook her up more than the abduction scene. She gave Eva a side hug and turned to go to her room.

"Wait." Eva grabbed two cookies, placed them on a napkin, and handed them to Tina.

Tina's throat closed with the need to cry. She nodded, forced a smile, and waved a goodbye. When she got to her room, she handed the cookies to Scout. Her cookies from earlier had turned to sawdust in her mouth. She'd be staying away from snickerdoodles forever.

She tossed her purse onto her bed and yanked her coat off. Something in her pocket banged her knee. How could she forget the present?

Sitting on the edge of the bed, she pulled the bright package out. She chewed on her lip as she twisted the small box in her hands. Part of her wanted to toss it across the room. The bigger part wanted to believe that Susan still cared for her.

With shaky fingers, she pulled the ribbon and slid her finger under the tape. Inside the box, nestled in tissue paper, sat a silver necklace with a dog that looked a lot like Scout, though it was more likely a German Shepherd. How had Susan known?

Scout slinked up, his nose going haywire, twitching this way and that. He sniffed at the box, then the paper. A low growl rumbled from him, and he pawed at the wrappings.

Tina's heart slowed at the clear signal Scout was sending. Scout only acted like this when he was trying to tell her something.

She dug her phone out of her purse and dialed Susan. "Hey, Susan. It's Tina." Tina cringed.

"Oh, hi, honey." A muffled shush came from Susan's end.

"I wanted to thank you for the necklace. It's beautiful."

"Oh, well, yes, you're welcome." Susan's distracted tone brought the tears Tina had fought so hard to push down right back up. "Actually, Blake picked it out. I ... I couldn't get out and asked him to buy something for you. He said you have a dog now."

"Blake bought it?"

"Yeah. Sorry I didn't pick it out myself." A crash sounded in Susan's house. "Oh, I've got to go. Talk to you later, Tina."

The call disconnected, and Tina stared at the phone. If she focused on Susan's treatment, Tina's heart would break. So, she zeroed in on Blake and Scout's continued signs toward him. Was he up to no good or in some kind of trouble? There was one way to find out.

"Come on, Scout." Tina strode to her door with determined steps. "We're going for a drive."

NINETEEN

"Hey, Tina. It's Milo." Milo paced on his mom's porch, shivering as a frigid wind blasted through his coat.

"Hey." Her hesitant tone fortified his resolve for calling.

"Listen, I just wanted to apologize again for what I said at the tree farm." Milo speared his hand through his hair. "I shouldn't have taken my frustration out on you. You and Scout have been amazing, a real help to the case."

"Don't worry about it, Milo." Tina sighed. "I live on a ranch full of moody guys. I get it. It's ... it's just bad timing."

"Okay."

What the heck did that mean? Bad timing for her to show up at the scene or bad timing for them?

"Want to—"

"Listen, Milo," Tina talked over him. "I need to go."

"All right."

"Thanks for the call."

The call died before he could say goodbye. He looked up at the stars, frustration building along his shoulders. Was that the blowoff of the century? Had his controlling attitude pushed her away?

Jase always complained of Milo keeping too tight a grip on life and others. Could that be why Jase hadn't told Milo of his change in career choice? Why his mom hadn't told him she'd started dating again? Would the world fall apart if he loosened up?

Maybe.

Wow. Was he really that egocentric?

The wind pelted him with icy air, pushing him to go inside. He trudged back into his mom's house, where she and Stone were busy making dinner. Stone slammed the knife into a carrot, and the vegetable rolled off the counter and onto the floor.

"Easy movements, Jeff." Mom laughed as she grabbed the carrot and rinsed it in the sink. "You don't have to attack the poor thing."

The pink in her cheeks and the soft smile on her face as she handed Stone the carrot settled in Milo's chest. He was happy his mom had finally moved on. Eleven years was more than enough time for her to grieve.

"I told you, Mags." Stone took her hand, instead of the carrot. "I'm no good in the kitchen."

"Well ... " She held his gaze, and Milo felt like he was intruding. "We'll just have to change that."

Milo slowed his approach. "Listen, why don't I head home?"

"No." His mom stepped back from Stone and placed her hands on her hips. "I've hardly seen you since

Thanksgiving weekend. You are staying, and that's an order."

She spun on her heel and stomped to stir the meat browning on the stove. How could she make him feel like he was seven again? Stone snorted a laugh, his mouth pressed tightly closed.

"Guess you're staying." He lifted an eyebrow. "Sit. Something's up. Might as well spill it."

Milo slumped on to the stool at the counter with a sigh. "I think I screwed it up with Tina."

"What happened?" Stone asked as he concentrated hard on slicing the carrot.

"Today, at the tree farm, I barked at her. Told her she hadn't been any help."

Mom gasped, spinning around with the wooden spoon shaking at him. "Milo Jacob Bishop, how could you say such a thing?"

"I know. I know." He cringed, hoping she didn't whack him. "The father of the latest child had just reamed us, and my frustration bubbled out on Tina." He closed his eyes at the memory of her flinching. "I apologized immediately. Just called her again, but she blew me off. Said 'It's just bad timing.' What does that even mean?"

"Oh, honey." Mom crossed the kitchen and leaned on the counter beside Stone.

"Maybe it's better this way. Less distracting." Did Milo mean that? He felt like the Grinch, his heart too small, leaving emptiness where the organ should be.

"Bishop, you need to give her time. She's been through a lot." Stone laid the knife down on the cutting board. "She was always quiet. Not necessarily shy, just ... cautious. Always examining people like she searched for their true motives. Probably because of her real parents."

"That poor girl." Mom tsked, slid the cutting board across the counter, and with efficient movements, sliced the carrots.

All the things Tina had said about her past came shuffling back to the forefront of his mind. He hadn't wanted to imagine what life had been like for her, but it always skimmed under the surface of his thoughts.

"I'm surprised she didn't catch on to John, her foster father, before." Stone cringed. "Not that any of us noticed he was a monster."

Mom patted Stone on the sleeve. "It wasn't your fault, either."

"Don't give up on her, Milo." Stone leaned his arms on the counter. "People have been doing that her whole life. If you think there might be something between you two, you need to pursue her, man. Don't let her hesitance stop you."

There was something there. She'd enthralled him from the moment she leaned over him in the wilderness, her cheeks pink with cold and worry in her eyes. He also didn't want to push, to be the control freak he knew he'd been in the past.

"I don't know. I don't want to ramrod my way in. I've done that enough in my life." Milo picked at a loose string on the Christmas placemat decorating the counter.

"Honey, it doesn't have to be a ramrod. Maybe just a gentle nudge." Mom stilled his hand with hers. "Jeff is right, though. Through other peoples' actions, she's been told she doesn't matter." Mom's forehead scrunched, her voice thick with sadness. "From what I've been told, it sounds like the only ones who ever really cared about her were her foster sister and foster mom, and we all know how that ended."

"Susan, her foster mom, loved those kids like they were her own." Stone slid his hand across Mom's shoulders.

"Still," Mom huffed with a shrug, "Tina needs encouragement, Milo, just like all of us do." She peeked up at Stone with a secret smile on her face, before turning back to Milo. "She just might need more encouragement than others."

Now, he not only was getting relationship advice from his boss, but also his mom? He'd take it. When it came to Tina, he felt like he was rushing down the Colorado River rapids without a life vest. If someone was willing to throw him a lifeline, he'd grab on tight with both hands.

TWENTY

"I can't believe it still works."

Tina stared at her phone as the circle with Blake's picture from high school stared back at her. She glanced up at Blake's truck sitting in the parking lot of the rundown apartments, the same apartments Samantha had told Tina about living in. When she had clicked the *Life360* app Susan had made them all load onto their phones as teenagers, she hadn't expected it to actually show where Blake was.

Tina settled into her seat and dug through the Vicco's Charcoalburger Drive-in bag for her fries. How pathetic was it that they both still had their phones from school? Was that evidence of her and Blake's poor existence since leaving the Harris house or proof that Susan's insistence on teaching them frugality had worked?

Tina sighed, as her thoughts wandered through the Christmases since leaving the Harris's. Her life was like this rundown apartment complex. Christmas lights lined a few windows with joy, but the rest sat dark. Dreary.

She shoved a fry into her mouth and dug out her chili cheese elk burger. *Tina, I'm so sorry.* The words from Faith's letter sprang to mind and stung her nose. *I wish we could have the life we whispered about together late into the night. I'm just not strong enough.*

Tina shook her head, the apartment lights blurring. Faith was the strongest person Tina had ever known. *I need you to do me a favor. Live life for both of us. Forgive the past, the people, yourself, me. Don't let our past wrap its evil hands around you like I have. You are going to make this world better. I know it. So, please, find a life that's filled with love and joy. You deserve it. We all do.*

Tina had failed Faith — let the darkness of unforgiveness cinch tight around Tina's heart. Hadn't she kept others at a distance so she couldn't be hurt? Even after finding friends at the ranch whose loyalty couldn't be questioned, she'd run away, choosing a cold, forlorn Thanksgiving rather than the warmth of the makeshift family.

Now, she might have driven Milo away, too. Why had she said it was bad timing and cut the call off? She'd meant the call had been bad timing, but the way she'd said it implied more. Why would she push him away when he'd not only shown interest but also hadn't shied away from her past? That wasn't living the life she and Faith had wanted. That was intentionally keeping her existence dark and desolate, like most of the apartment windows.

She didn't want to live in the shadow of the past anymore.

She wanted a life filled with light and merriment.

Wanted a life worth celebrating.

Scout whined in his kennel in the back. Why'd she put him back there? She needed his comfort, but getting out now would reveal her location. Maybe staking out Blake's place wasn't the smartest idea.

"I know, buddy." She turned in her seat and peered through the crate. "We'll take a break soon. We'll go for a walk before we come back."

Scout's tail thumped against the enclosure, pulling a smile upon her face. She turned back around, leaning her head against the seat as a spark of hope flickered in her heart. Hadn't life been getting better since she took the job at Stryker? Maybe finding joy wouldn't be as hard as she thought.

Movement pulled her attention to the second story. She slouched further down in her seat. Silly, since she had parked in the dark to hide. Blake passed under the light, his head turning this way and that as he dashed down the steps. The pounding of her heart climbed up her throat. The fries hardened to bricks in her stomach.

"Here we go," she whispered to herself as Blake pulled out of his parking spot and sped from the lot.

She waited until he turned on to the road, then turned the key in the ignition. She glanced at the app. Blake's face bubble moved down the street toward the interstate. She didn't want to take the chance of the app losing him, but she also couldn't give her position away. Why hadn't she taken lessons in stalking?

She pulled onto the road with one car between them. Her slick palms slipped on the steering wheel. A sigh of relief leaked out when he continued under the overpass toward the south side of town instead of getting on the interstate.

She flipped the heater off as sweat dripped down her back. Was she this stressed when the bomb had been strapped to her car? Probably more, but it was close. Her mind raced as he pulled into Susan's neighborhood.

"Why is he stopping here?" Her voice was loud in the car as she cut her lights and slowly inched toward her old home.

Blake had parked across the street, away from the streetlight. Tina pulled in behind a vehicle three houses down. The longer Blake sat in his truck, the greater the tension built along Tina's spine. She shouldn't be here by herself. If he was doing something illegal, she had no clue how to stop him alone.

Sure, she had Scout, but she'd never worked with him to apprehend suspects. He'd done that kind of stuff in the Army, but Tina didn't know how to command him. She took out her phone, determined to trust others, to reach out to friends who cared for her.

TWENTY-ONE

Milo stared at his computer, his eyes blurring and a headache building at his temples. He should go to bed instead of looking through the evidence for the abductions for the millionth time. Nothing had changed since that afternoon, or that morning, or the morning before.

He clicked over to the surveillance feed of the day downtown, his heart picking up when Tina and Scout entered the screen. Okay. He was officially pathetic, watching a video just to catch a glimpse of her. He clicked the window closed with a huff of disgust and pushed back from his dining room table.

Maybe he should just call her and ask what she meant by that bad timing remark? He glanced at his watch and groaned. He'd have to wait until the morning. He couldn't call her this late. Or could he?

He growled and speared his hands through his hair, giving it a hard yank. Why did she make him feel like he was in high school again — all self-conscious and unsure? He dropped his arms with a sigh.

She sparked something in him, like that wonderful warmth he got from drinking Mom's homemade cocoa sitting by the Christmas tree with a fire crackling low in the fireplace — the warmth of hope and the promise of the thrill of Christmas morning.

He wouldn't let himself get buried in his work and misplaced obligations anymore. He pulled his phone from his pocket, staring at the black screen. The phone vibrated in his hand, causing him to jump and drop it. Scooping it up, his eyes widened at Tina's picture on the screen.

"Hello?" His voice cracked, and he cleared it, his neck and ears heating.

"Milo?" Tina's voice was hushed and airy. Was she as nervous to call as he had been?

"Yeah. I'm glad you called, T—"

"I need your help." Her rushed words froze in his gut.

"Where are you? What's wrong?" He snatched his sidearm off the table and grabbed his coat as he stalked to his garage.

"Scout acted weird with the present Susan gave me. When I called her, she said Blake got it for me." Tina's nervous tone spiked his body with adrenaline. "Remember how Scout growled at Blake outside that store?"

"Yeah."

"Scout barked at him earlier today from his kennel. Actually barked." Tina's pause nearly made him lose it. "Scout never does that, so I decided to find Blake and follow him."

"You did what?" Milo cringed as he practically

shouted into the phone. "Sorry." He gripped the steering wheel of his Dodge Power Wagon as he sped down his street. "Tina, where are you?"

"I'm down the street from Susan's house. Do you remember where that is?"

"Yeah."

His fingers eased their death grip. Thank God Milo had bought a house close to his mom's. Tina was only fifteen blocks away.

"What is Blake doing?"

"Just sitting in his truck. He parked it across the street." Tina sighed. "I don't understand. Why would he come over here then just sit outside?"

"I'm close. I'll be right there."

"He's getting out." Tina's voice hitched with anticipation. "He's crossing to Susan's house. I'm going to get closer."

"No, Tina."

The phone went dead. Milo punched the gas pedal down further, rocketing him down the winding neighborhood roads. He dialed Callahan.

"You better have a good reason for calling me at midnight, Bishop." Callahan sounded like her normal grumpy self, so Milo didn't worry. Besides, she lived closer than anyone else he could think of at the moment.

"I need you to meet me at Susan Harris's house on Bennett. Address might be under the name John Harris." Milo rattled off. "I may have a situation I need your help with."

"Got it. Be right there."

Milo tossed his phone onto the seat. Why hadn't

Tina listened to him and waited? His truck fishtailed across the winter street as he turned the corner too fast.

Why had she called him and not her friends at Stryker? Hope tried to push the fear aside, but the choking panic kept its grip on his throat. When they cleared up whatever mess she'd found, he would convince her their timing was anything but bad.

TWENTY-TWO

Heart racing, Tina darted up the front yard to the corner of the house. Her pulse roared loud in her ears, drowning out all other noise. She leaned her head against the house, closed her eyes, and willed her heart to slow down.

Should she have waited for Milo? She clenched her hand around Scout's leash. What if Blake did something while she waited? No, she couldn't wait and risk that. She and Scout could probably take care of Blake on their own. She leaned to peek around the corner, her heart almost choking her as it pounded in her throat.

Did she really want to go alone?

"I told you to wait." Milo's harsh whisper behind her raised a scream up her throat.

She clamped her hand over her mouth and swallowed the sound down, turning her back against the house. Scout leaned against Milo's leg, a look of adoration, possibly relief, across his furry face. *Traitor*.

Milo leaned closer, pulling her to him so his mouth was close to her ear. "You scared me to death."

The hot air against her skin sent shivers down her spine and warmth through her system. She was strong enough to face uncertainty alone, she'd been doing it all of her life. Yet, she didn't have to anymore. She had her friends at the ranch, and she had Milo.

"What's going on here?" Milo whispered again, pulling her back to reality.

He scanned the area as she leaned up to him. She let the citrus and cedar smell that clung to him ease her.

"Blake went around the corner towards the back of the house. There's a gate there to the backyard." She swallowed at the thought of the pitch-black side yard, relieved Milo was there. "I was about to peek to see if he was there when you snuck up on me."

He flashed her a smile before scanning the neighborhood again. He motioned to a car that stopped across the street, then turned an intense gaze on her. He grabbed the collar of her coat and pulled her close.

"You and Scout lead. I'll cover you."

He was trusting her? He wasn't forcing her behind him? Heat rushed to her cold fingers, leaving them tingly. He leaned down and pressed a hard, quick kiss to her lips. Her heart picked up speed for an entirely different reason.

"I'm glad you called me." His breathless words strengthened her resolve.

"Me, too." Two words had never held such weight.

"Okay, let's go."

Tina's eyes widened as a woman rushed across the

street towards them, her gun drawn. Milo must've called in backup. Hopefully, they wouldn't need it. She prayed this was all a misunderstanding.

Tina leaned around the corner and squinted into the darkness. Nothing, unless Blake had found a way to squeeze himself behind the bare rose bushes and was hiding. She let Scout off the leash.

"Scout, find Blake." She pulled the gift wrap from Susan's present out of her pocket and extended it to Scout.

The dog beelined to the wooden gate and sat, looking at the latch. Tina stood off to the side, the tall security fence stretching above her, not sure what to do. Should she open the gate and, what? Breach the backyard? The woman stopped on the opposite side of the entrance, nodded once at Tina with confidence, then glanced at Milo. Tina followed her lead and turned to Milo crowding against her.

He did some hand motions that made no sense. The woman signaled in return. Milo leaned over.

"You open the gate with the cord. We'll clear th—"

The latch clicked. Milo tensed against her side. As the gate swung towards the backyard, Milo, his friend, and Scout rushed through the opening like they'd coordinated the assault.

The security light flashed on over the fence. A grunt sounded through the wood. Tina took a deep breath and entered the backyard.

"Wait. I've done nothing wrong." Blake's hoarse whisper caused a prickling on her scalp.

Milo's friend had Blake pinned to the ground. "Then why are you sneaking around in the dark?"

"I ... I thought something was going on with my foster mom. I wanted to check first before I called it in." He froze when Scout sniffed his head.

"You thought something was going on?" Milo asked, his voice pitched low.

Scout's nose lifted, sniffing the air. His head whipped toward the yard, his tail thumping. Tina scanned the area, dread pooling in her stomach. Her hands lost all feeling as Scout dashed deeper into the yard. Her gaze darted from one toy to another as Scout zigzagged across the snow.

"Milo." Her voice croaked, barely making it around the lump lodged in her throat.

Milo glanced up at her, then turned to follow her gaze. The light in the living room snapped on and brightened the yard even further. Tina moved toward the sliding glass door without thinking. She reached it just as the glass whooshed open.

"Tina?" Susan stood, her hand holding the top of her tattered bubblegum pink robe closed, her eyebrows hitching to her graying hair.

"Mom, what have you done?" Tina stifled the sob that choked her as Scout dashed into the house.

Susan gasped, then shrieked as Tina pushed past her. Susan grabbed Tina's hair and pulled, snapping her head back.

"They're mine." Susan's shrill tone rose all the hairs on Tina's neck. "They need me. Their parents weren't even watching them. I can take better care of them." Desperation clung to Susan's words.

Tina spun and knocked Susan's grip free, ripping a fist of hair out with a painful yank. Susan stumbled backwards into Milo. He grabbed her arms as she twisted and screamed about how they were hers. Her face contorted into tortured expressions.

Scout whined, and Tina rushed through the house to the back bedroom where Scout pawed at the door. She turned the knob, her lips and chin quivering as she held her breath. Light from the hallway spilled into the room, illuminating four trembling children huddled against the wall.

TWENTY-THREE

"I just don't understand why she'd do something like this?" Tina said for the fourth time since they'd found the children at her foster mom's house.

Milo didn't know how to answer. Tina clung to a paper cup of coffee, still full and no longer steaming. She stared at the families across the precinct as they cried, clinging to each other. Milo still tried to process that Susan Harris had stolen the children. He leaned against the desk beside Tina, took the coffee cup from her grip, and slid his hand across her back.

"I think, maybe, she was just lonely." He wrapped his arm around Tina when she leaned her head onto his shoulder. "The anniversary of Faith's death was right before Thanksgiving. That must have been the stressor that pushed her over."

"I should've gone over more, shouldn't have pushed her away." Tina's voice had lost all its normal power. "I didn't even know she'd kept her father's car."

Tina had felt terrible when they'd found the Outback

parked in Susan's garage. Since Susan's father had been put in a nursing home up valley almost two years before, Tina hadn't thought about him or what had happened to his stuff. With the car registered in Pitkin County and the last name not matching Susan's, Milo probably never would've made the connection.

"We all did things we shouldn't have." Blake strode up from Stone's office, his shoulders slumped. "But her actions are not your fault, Tina. None of this has ever been your fault."

"Yours either, son." Stone clapped a hand on Blake's shoulder. "You've done excellent work here, Blake. I'm glad you've joined the team."

Blake nodded once and crossed his arms. Did he even hear the praise in Stone's voice? Milo shook his head. Blake's pained expression said he didn't.

"Team?" Tina asked the question burning on Milo's tongue.

"Blake has been working undercover. I snagged him from the Denver narcotics department." Stone tipped his head at Blake. "His work there gave him access to the Marcot gang."

"We've been investigating them for months." Milo hated feeling like he was in the dark. He'd be questioning Stone later about keeping him and Callahan out of the loop.

"I'm in." Blake shrugged. "And you bringing me to the precinct in handcuffs hopefully reinforced my cover."

"You're working undercover with a drug ring?" Tina bit her lip. "Isn't that dangerous?"

Blake's mouth tipped into a one-sided grin. "Yeah."

He sobered. "I think it's why your dog hates me. The stench of drugs cling to clothing."

"But ... but..." Tina's stutter lightened Milo's mood. "Won't they get suspicious since you've been hanging out with Jase and stuff?"

"Nah. That's my cover." Blake rubbed his neck. "Word on the street is the cops got too close for comfort in Denver, so I ventured home to hook into the growing scene here."

"It's worked out so far." Stone motioned to Tina. "You did great tonight. Think you might want to join the team, too? We could use a pair like you and Scout."

Stone was full of surprises tonight. Milo squeezed Tina's arm. While he would love to work with her every day, he wasn't sure if he could handle seeing her in danger either.

"Me?" Tina gulped before shaking her head. "No. No, thank you. I like my place out at Stryker."

"I get that, and I'm happy you've found a home." Stone grumbled, not sounding happy at all.

"But we'll come help whenever you need us." Tina leaned into Milo with a sigh. "What's ... what's going to happen to Susan?"

"It won't be good." Milo didn't want to keep anything from Tina. "Kidnapping is a felony. Even with the kids unharmed, it could be anywhere between eight and life in prison, depending on what the attorneys of the families try to push for."

"She might be able to plead insanity." Stone looked down the hall toward the holding cells. "We'll just have to see how the evidence stacks up."

"Poor Susan." Tina sniffed, wringing her hands together. "Is there anything I can do to help her?"

"You can be there for her." Stone gave Tina the look Milo knew well, the one that said Stone was about to unload a whopper of a lesson.

"Show her you love her." Stone cleared his throat. "Show her that John's sins haven't tainted her family. That you, the both of you, haven't left her." He glanced from Tina to Blake. "I'm not excusing what she's done, but all she ever wanted was a family with lots of kids." He waved towards the children. "John tore that from her, just like he tore something from every one of you."

Tina shuddered under Milo's arm as Stone's words settled in Milo's gut. He scooted closer and wrapped his arm around her waist, needing her near. Had he allowed his father's murder to tear life from him as well? He thought about the months and years he'd spent focusing on his duties, pushing relationships aside for the sake of his goals.

"The two of you can support Susan by living a life of love she only ever found in you kids." Stone rubbed his hand over his short hair. "You can find the happiness she always wanted to give you."

Isn't that what Milo's father would want Milo to do, too? Find the joy and love Dad had found in life with Mom? He wouldn't want Milo to miss out by filling the void of father and provider left by his dad's death. He'd want Milo finding reasons to celebrate life.

Tina wrapped her arm around Milo's back and twisted her fingers into the side of his sweatshirt. The tension of the night—no, the last ten years unfurled its fist around his gut. He held Tina tight as she talked. He'd found reason to shed his self-imposed duty and celebrate. That reason was about five-two, with blonde hair that framed her beautiful face, brown eyes tinted like the red stone that covered the mountains, and smelled of candy canes and a tinge of dog.

TWENTY-FOUR

The day after Christmas, Tina sucked on the tiny candy cane as she hiked to meet Milo at top of the Red Mountain Trail. He'd called an hour and a half ago, saying he needed her help and to bring Scout. She'd grabbed her survival pack she'd restocked after her Thanksgiving trip and rushed out of the house.

As the lights in the valley blinked on below her and the sky turned from light blush pink to dark flamingo, she worried she hadn't hiked fast enough to be any help. She drew in a frigid breath as her lungs threatened to explode with her fast climb up the mountain. Night would ruin her chance to safely follow Scout as he searched for whoever had gotten themselves lost on the iconic trail. The gigantic lighted cross that marked the end of the main path and could be seen from the valley below loomed ahead as she rounded a turn.

"Come on, Scout. We're almost there." She forced the words out, though the dog didn't need any encouragement from her.

As she crested the ridge to the clearing at the cross's base, she skidded, almost tripping over her feet. Christmas lights blinked from where they were threaded through the sagebrush and cedar trees. Soft Christmas music played from speakers somewhere. A fire burned low on top of the snow, and Milo sat on one of two logs set up like seats warming his hands.

Scout barked, jerking Milo's head up. Tina's heart stopped in her chest as his gaze connected with hers. There wasn't someone lost? Milo stood, the log tipping at his sudden movement and rolling a few feet away.

"You made it." Milo closed the distance between them in five large steps and stopped just short of taking her in his arms.

Oh, how she wished he would.

He smiled crookedly. "What took you so long?"

She snorted, adjusting the pack on her back. "You try hiking up this trail in the fading light carrying a fifty-pound bag."

His eyes twinkled in the soft Christmas lights. "I did." He wrapped his hand around her pack's strap and pulled it off. "And dragged a sled full of firewood. All these cedars are too green for a decent fire."

He set the pack down and reached for her hand. She stared at him. What should she say? Questions jumbled against each other, making her brain a complete mess.

She squeezed his hand before dropping it and stepping toward the middle of the opening. She needed a second to catch her breath and make sense of what was happening.

"So, you did all this?" She pointed to the brush.

"Yeah." He lifted one shoulder. "I found some battery-operated lights. Thought it'd be romantic." He chuckled, dropping his head and rubbing his neck. "I'm not sure what I'm doing here."

"Well, it's romantic all right." Tina turned in a circle and gasped at Glenwood Springs, lighted like a beautiful Christmas tree below. "It's over the top romantic."

"Even though I led you to believe you were going on a search?" Milo took a step closer.

"Yeah." Tina tried to stifle her smile as she eyed him. "It's a nice alternative."

"Even though you had to hike three miles up a snow-covered trail?" His next move diminished the distance between them, making her nerves zip like the electricity racing through the giant cross.

"That, I might not be so forgiving of."

Her breath caught as he reached up and tucked her hair behind her ear. Her knees almost buckled as his fingers trailed down her neck. He reached into his pocket with his other hand, and Tina almost hyperventilated.

Please don't be a box. Please don't be a box.

As much as she liked Milo, that would be moving way too fast for her liking.

"Relax." His lips pressed together like he was trying not to laugh. "It's just a remote."

He pulled out a small rectangle, and the music changed, getting louder. The first few notes of Lee Ann Womack's *What Are You Doing New Year's Eve* brought tears to her eyes. How had he known?

He rubbed his forehead with his fist and took a step back. "Shoot. I screwed up. What did I do wrong?"

She grabbed his hand to stop his retreat. "This was Faith's favorite Christmas song."

Milo fumbled in his pocket. "I'll change it."

"No." Tina pulled his other arm. "Dance with me?"

"That's what I'd hoped for, but now—"

"It's perfect."

She pulled his arms around her waist and wrapped hers around his shoulders. She tucked her face into his neck, liking the slight slope that gave her a boost in height and relished his heat against her chilled nose and cheeks. They swayed to the slow song, so different from most Christmas songs. He pulled her tight so not even air could get between them.

"I could never figure out why Faith liked this song so much. I'd tease her every time she played it." Her lips brushed against his skin as she spoke, tempting her to press a kiss there. "She said it was a song of hope-filled tomorrows, of happiness beyond the excitement of Christmas." The memory, while still painful, also filled Tina with joy. "I get it now. I get what Faith always wanted me to see."

Giving into temptation, she pressed a kiss to his pulse. She pulled back enough to peer into his eyes. He leaned down with excruciating slowness, the anticipation of his kiss building warmth in her belly.

Scout bumped into the back of Tina's legs, pushing her the rest of the way. Milo's lips connected with hers, laughter mingling with the touch. How could she have ever thought happiness wasn't meant for her? She stood on her tiptoes and dived in for another.

After the song had played to the end and repeated

half through, Milo pulled back, leaning his forehead to hers. Her arms tingled with renewed adrenaline and her legs jiggled like a bowl full of jelly. His ragged breath held a hint of hot chocolate. Had he lugged food up here as well?

"So, Tasty Tina." He smirked. "In the words of Lee Ann, what are you doing New Year's Eve?"

"Hopefully, holding you good and tight."

His triumphant smile stretched across his face as he ran his thumb along her chin. Yeah, she was ready to celebrate life again. Ready to trust that she could be happy and find love. She pulled him down to her as the song played again.

TWENTY-FIVE

"So, how's the new roommates working out for you, Tasty?" Rafe tossed a card into the discard pile and held two fingers up to Jake.

"Stop calling me that." Tina glared at Rafe over the table, then glanced at Lena Rebel, who was talking to Jase at the kitchen island. "Lena's great. A little intense and crankier than my last roommates, but I'm glad she moved out here to join us." Tina winked at Kiki squished between Rafe and Derrick. "And Kiki's a blast. I think it'll work out fine."

"I still can't believe Zeke and Samantha sprung that whole wedding on us Christmas Day." Rafe set his cards face down on the table and crossed his arms. "Then, just took Eva and jetted away to who knows where."

"The lifestyle of the super-rich." Derrick shuffled his cards in his hands. "Leaves us poor folks behind to suffer."

"Like you're living in squalor." Tina snorted,

knowing the guys made bank working for Zeke. "And you all get to jet off all the time."

"That's work, and it's different." Derrick pointed his cards at her.

"Worst part was they took Eva. Whoever heard of taking a kid on a honeymoon?" Jake scowled as he threw his hand into the discard pile. "I fold."

Milo laughed a rich, deep sound that curled all the way to Tina's toes. "You guys look like someone stole your puppy or something."

"No, not their puppy, just their princess." Kiki grimaced at her cards, her eyebrows squished together as she shifted them around.

Derrick leaned over, pointed at her cards, and whispered something in her ear. Tina stifled a smile as Kiki's eyes lit up, knowing full well the day trader didn't have any trouble with strategy. Someday, those two would have to come to grips with the attraction that they kept firmly banked.

Milo's arm stretched across Tina's shoulders, and his fingers toyed with her hair. Every soft tug shot sparks straight to her stomach. How could such a simple touch build so much heat?

"Enough chitchat. Let's finish this hand, so I can show you my surprise." Rafe smiled like a kid up to no good.

Everyone laid down their cards, but Tina held hers, building the anticipation. The sizable pot on this hand would last her half a year, at least. She bit her lip to keep the smile in, her gaze darting to everyone who'd become her family. Joy bubbled up from her toes, making her lightheaded.

"The princess may be gone." Tina laid down her four queens and an ace with a flourish. "But there are plenty of queens left."

The guys groused and moaned in their various fashions that had become so familiar to Tina. She loved how they lost in exaggerated ways, whether they were playing cards, shooting guns, or running training ops. It was how she always pictured a family would act together.

"Enough of this." Rafe stood. "You all head out to the porch. It's about time for my New Year's Eve gift."

Tina stretched forward and scooped all the miniature candy canes from the middle of the table into her pile. She could make these babies last a long time. Milo leaned over and kissed right below her ear. A delicious shiver skated across her skin.

"Long live the queen," he whispered in her ear, kissing her again, before pulling her out of her seat. "Come on. We don't want to miss Rafe's surprise."

"I don't know." Tina shrugged, and she stuck her arms into her coat that Milo held up. "Kissing you is probably better than any surprise Rafe could come up with."

Milo stared into her eyes, the look full of promise. "There will be plenty of time for that, too."

He gave her a peck too quick for her liking, grabbed her hand, and pulled her outside. Everyone gathered on the porch, bundled against the frosty night in their coats. Some weird synthesized piano music from way before her time blared over the speakers.

"Nice." Milo wrapped his arms around her and

pulled her back against him. *"The Final Countdown* by Europe."

Tina shook her head. How did he even know that? Another set of synthetic sounds layered upon the first, building the drama Rafe so loved. Drums joined the mix, and fireworks exploded from the field beyond the backyard.

Tina jumped, then laughed as Milo tightened his hold.

"He better have gotten a permit," Milo grumbled behind her.

She leaned her head back against his chest with a sigh as brilliant colors popped in the starry sky, reflecting off the frozen pond the guys kept ready for ice skating. Could the night be any more perfect?

"Here's to a New Year." Milo whispered in her ear, kissing her on the head. "I have a feeling it's going to be a great one."

For the first time in her life, Tina wholeheartedly agreed. She threaded her fingers through his as the firework show boomed on. It was the perfect way to celebrate a life of hope-filled tomorrows.

Want to know what happens on the Stryker Ranch next? Grab Crashing Into Jake directly from the author and save. For a thrilling adventure and toe-curling romance in the snow-covered Colorado mountains, don't miss the next Stryker book.

EXCERPT FROM CRASHING INTO JAKE

Jake Silva yanked his hand away from where he

rubbed his knee. He'd twisted the prosthetic bottom half while playing chase with his boss's stepdaughter, Evangeline, earlier, and his knee still ached. The last thing he needed was for the others to witness him nursing it. The worry he'd see in the women's expressions would pinch, but it would be the guilt he saw in his brothers-in-arms that would turn Jake's contented mood dark.

"Uncle Jake, you stopped reading." Eva peered up at him from where she leaned against his side.

"Sorry, honey. I got distracted."

He'd already read *Beauty and the Beast* to her three times in the last thirty minutes, yet here he still sat, regaling the precious four-year-old of how Belle's love changed the beastly prince. He wished Eva still obsessed over *Sleeping Beauty*. That book didn't hit so close to home. It wasn't like the rambunctious girl to stay on one princess for long though, not when there were so many to choose from.

Eva ran her hand down the picture with a dramatic sigh. "What do you think your princess will look like?"

"My princess?" Jake forced his voice to not turn gruff. "I thought you were my princess."

Eva turned so she sat on her knees facing him, her little fists plopped on her hips. She screwed her face up into what he imagined she thought was mean, but really was just adorable. Man, he loved this girl. The last few months since she and her mother had showed up brought a light to the pit he'd spiraled into.

"Now you wisten to me, and you wisten to me now, mister." Where did she come up with this stuff? "You are a handsome prince, just like the beast."

She slammed her chubby finger on the picture of the beast hidden in shadows. He should stick to the shadows as well. Few wanted the reminder his scarred face gave. He shook his head and focused on Eva.

"Don't shake your head at me. I need cousins and lots of them."

Jake choked on spit as he inhaled sharply. "Cousins?"

"Yes. If you get married, you'll have babies, then I'll get cousins."

"I don't think anyone will want ugly ol' me as a prince. Besides, I'm too cranky." He tweaked her nose, hoping to distract her. "But go tell Sosimo about your plan. He's already found and married his princess. You should tell them to hurry up."

Eva climbed onto his lap and put her tiny hands on both of his cheeks. The sorrow that pooled in her sparkling blue eyes nearly made him promise to rush off to wherever women hung out these days and round himself up a wife.

"You are not ugly or cranky. Don't talk mean like that. It's not nice."

What a jerk he was. "I'm sorry, sweetheart. I didn't mean to hurt your feelings."

"You're pretty and nice, and I love you, Uncle Jake." She threw her arms around his neck and squeezed tightly.

He held her and closed his eyes, glad for the moment to get the giant ball of emotion unstuck from his throat. The day his former Sergeant Major and now boss, Zeke Greene, had fallen and fallen hard for Eva's mother had been the day that hope for a new tomorrow peeked into his heart. While he still wasn't sure he could ever move past the ghosts that haunted him at night and be safe enough for a wife to be around, having women and children at the ranch helped him think less often of all he'd lost in the last mission he'd fought for the US Army.

One would think it would've done the opposite, since all he had ever wanted was to serve his country with honor and marry someone who would be his rock to come home to. It was a family legacy that had started with his grandfather, one he'd wanted more than anything. But one mission, one moment in time, had shredded all his dreams to dust. At least here he could live vicariously through his friends' lives, being a part of a family unit that had no blood ties.

Rafe rushed into the room, a crease marring his normally jovial face. "Hey, Fairy Princess, I need to steal Uncle Jake away for important hero business. Why don't you go find Tina? I think she's working with that new dog of hers."

"Yeah!" Eva jumped in Jake's lap, kissing him loudly on his scarred cheek before jumping down and racing off. "Be safe, my brave knights."

"We will, my fair lady." Rafe waved to her and turned to Jake. "We're heading to Steamboat. Can you be ready to fly in ten?"

Jake nodded, his heart picking up with the intensity Rafe exuded. "What's up?"

"Davis Field just called—"

"From the sandbox?" Wasn't Davis still overseas?

"Yeah. His baby sister is in some kind of trouble." Rafe speared his hand through his normally perfect hair.

"Well, I guess she's not a baby anymore, and it's more their cousin that's in trouble."

"Rafe, breathe, man. What do you know?"

"Some guy's been stalking Chloe, Davis's cousin. She's an up-and-coming country singer. She's in Steamboat for a music festival, and the creep followed them." Rafe headed toward the door. "You're flying us, and then you and I are playing babysitter."

Jake swallowed down his anxiety and followed Rafe out the door. He didn't mind his new job as part of Zeke's Stryker Security Force. Enjoyed it, surprisingly. The jobs he didn't like were the famous ones. They always looked at him funny, like they'd just bitten into a sour candy. Worst were the women that curled their bodies away in fear.

It shouldn't surprise him. Since his injury, he'd gotten that reaction from most women no matter where he went. No, Eva shouldn't get her hopes too high. He wouldn't be finding his princess anytime soon. Jake scowled as the joyful morning tanked to gloom.

Read *Crashing Into Jake* today!

ALSO BY SARA BLACKARD

Vestige in Time Series

Vestige of Power

Vestige of Hope

Vestige of Legacy

Vestige of Courage

Stryker Security Force Series

Mission Out of Control

Falling For Zeke

Capturing Sosimo

Celebrating Tina

Crashing Into Jake

Discovering Rafe

Convincing Derrick

Honoring Lena

Alaskan Rebels Series

A Rebel's Heart

A Rebel's Beacon

A Rebel's Promise

A Rebel's Trust

Wild Hearts of Alaska

Wild About Denali

Wild About Violet

Other Books
―――――――
Meeting Up with the Consultant

It was a mission like any other ... until it blew apart around them.

When the Army's Special Ops team is tasked with infiltrating the Columbian jungle and rescuing a kidnapped State Department family, the mission seems like every other one they've executed. But as the assignment unravels, not only is the mission's success at stake, but all the brothers-in-arms leaving the jungle alive hangs in the balance.

Mission Out of Control is the prequel short story for both Vestige in Hope and the Stryker Security Force Series.

ABOUT THE AUTHOR

Sara Blackard is an award-winning romance novelist who writes stories that thrill the imagination and strum heartstrings. When she's not crafting wild adventures and romances that make readers swoon, she's homeschooling her four adventurous boys and one fearless princess, keeping their off-grid house running (don't ask if it's clean), or enjoying the Alaskan lifestyle she and her Hunky Hubster love. Visit her website at shop.sarablackard.com